CHASE ME

A DRAGONS LOVE CURVES NOVEL

AIDY AWARD

Coffee Break Publishing

www.coffeebreakpublishing.com

Chase Me/ Aidy Award. -- 1st ed.

ASIN B0779RF557

ISBN 978-0-9904060-5-1

SHE'S STOLEN A PRICELESS RELIC FROM
HIS TREASURE, AND HIS HEART.

Ciara is the best damn wedding planner this side of anywhere,
but she's no thief.
That's exactly what the sexy-ass dragon shifter has accused
her of - stealing his treasure.
She's going to steal something of his all right—his sanity, if he
doesn't let her go so she can get back to giving couples their
happy ever afters.
It's the best way to ignore the fact she's sure she'll never get
one of her own.
Not with any man, or even a dragon.

Jakob is either going to kill the sexy, curvy woman who denies
she has The First Dragon's relic or take her to bed and drive
her as crazy as she's making him.
Why does he want her so much he can't even properly
interrogate her?
Might have something to do with the way his soul is
screaming at him to mark her, claim her, f*ck her, and make
dragon babies with her.

He can't give her his soul if she's already stolen it, or
something darker and more dangerous has.

For a lot of really Amazeballs people~

ACKNOWLEDGMENTS

I have a lot of people to thank for helping me get this book written and out into the world.

Thank you to Lyz Kelley for brainstorming with me. There were a few times I simply didn't know what happened next and you rocked my brain into figuring it out.

Special thanks to Hopey for going back through again and again to fix my typos. If there are still anymore left, they're totally my fault.

I really appreciate how my dad always, always believes that I can do it, whatever it is, and that he doesn't try to fix it, just gives me the pep talks to help me "git 'er dun."

I ran a contest for my Curvy Connection and Amazeballs to name a character. You rock Heather Rhodes for giving Wesley Alexander his name!

And as to the Amazeballs – you all are exactly that.

Thanks to those of you that cheered me on, proofread the book, told your friends all about it, and were so damned excited for this book to come out. You all are why I write books.

Hugs,
--A

Here there be dragons

—Really Old Maps

ALWAYS THE WEDDING PLANNER, NEVER THE BRIDE

*A*gh. Ciara's feet ached, her back was stiff and the headache she'd staved off with some ibuprofen four hours ago was rapidly creeping back behind her left eyeball. Nothing like the sweet pains of victory.

One more commission like this and she could afford to take that beach vacation she'd been promising Wesley for the past three years.

"Oh Sarah, there you are." The bride's mother, who was reason number one, two, three, and forty-three for said headache, waved her over. Mother-of-the-Bridezilla paid the bills, so Ciara pasted on her most helpful smile and greeted the table.

"Hello everyone. Having a nice time?"

Headache mom turned to the couple sitting next to her. "Bill, Thi, this is Sarah, the wedding planner. You simply must book her for your Linh's wedding. She is the best—always available for her clients. I called her last week at two in the morning when I simply knew that Bethany needed to have three more wedding cakes at the reception. Sarah never says no."

Oh, great. That's what she wanted to be known for. Being the slut of the wedding planner world.

"Well, I like to hear that. We want our baby to have everything she wants for her wedding. No expense spared. Do you have a card, Sarah?"

"It's Ciara actually, and yes, of course." She handed Bill, who she could already tell was wrapped around his daughter's little finger, a card. Bill handed the card to his wife. "Let me write your time and date on the back for you."

She pulled a pen out of her kit. Always prepared, true to her Girl Scout roots. She scribbled on the back of the card.

"Ciara Mosley-Willingham. Do you own Willingham Weddings, dear?"

Sigh. Not yet. Not ever if her mother had anything to do with it. "That honor goes to my mother, Wilhelmina."

"Ah, I see. Well, nepotism has its benefits." The table all chuckled at Bill's little joke.

Benefits schmenefits. If only they knew.

"I've got an appointment that just opened up for two weeks from Monday. Will that work to bring Linh in for a consultation?"

"Two weeks?"

She nodded. "I'm afraid the next available is in August."

The couple glanced at each other. They were not used to waiting, patiently. Most of her clients weren't.

"That's almost three months from now."

Headache mother raised a glass of champagne. "You wanted the best. Better get her while you can."

Thi raised an eyebrow, trying to intimidate Ciara. Not

gonna happen. Ciara gave the mother her award-winning account-getting smile.

Thi gave in. "We'll be there."

Bali with Wesley, here she comes. If she could ever get him to ask her out in the first place, and in another three years when her schedule cleared up. Not that her mother would ever allow her to take a vacation, but at least now she had a plan to get that date with the hunk of the office.

Ciara made her rounds, vying for a chance to run into Wes with the good news. News that should be celebrated, with a night on the town, a nice dinner, some satin sheets.

She checked in with the catering staff and found out he was in the kitchen. Wes, in a perfect three-piece suit with the purple pocket square and matching vest, just about took her breath away. How any man this good looking would be interested in her blew her mind.

By interested, she meant he flirted with her constantly at the office but hadn't ever asked her out. Ciara had made it perfectly clear she was willing and available.

He hinted, she smiled and nodded, and then nothing.

A girl could only wait so long for the man of her day dreams to make a move.

"Hey babe." He kissed her on the cheeks while holding his cell phone to his ear. "We've got a champagne shortage crisis on our hands."

No need to stress. Cool, calm, and collected. Always. "No problem. I'll bring in the secret back-up case I keep in my car."

Wes hung up his phone and winked at the disheveled waiter with the empty tray. "Told you Ciara would swing some of her magic."

He was such a sweet talker. She hoped he was a dirty talker too. Whoa, wait. Down girl. She had to get a date with him first. "I'll go grab it, but the bouquet toss is in a few minutes. Go chat up all the single girls and talk them into standing up to catch the bouquet."

One wink or an eyebrow waggle from him and they'd all be smashing each other in the face to catch those flowers whether they wanted to or not.

"I'll go get the champagne, you go catch the bouquet." Wes shook his head and shivered.

Lots of bouquets were in her future, but not for catching. Always the wedding planner, never the bride. Yet.

Here goes nothing, or something, or gah, just ask him.

"Hey, I just landed the Barton wedding. We should celebrate."

Wes grinned. "You are going to make us all zillionaires. I cannot even keep up."

Okay, this was going well. Ask him. "So, you'll go out with me to celebrate?"

"You bet."

He didn't hesitate even a little. She should have asked him months and months… and months ago.

"Are you free on Wednesday?" They had weddings on the weekends, but she hoped she didn't sound lame for suggesting a weeknight.

"Nope. But, I could do Thursday. Dinner, drinks, and I know the greatest place to go clubbing."

Dinner, drinks, and dancing. Perfect.

She wanted to jump up and down and clap her hands.

Not appropriate.

Be cool.

Ciara drew upon her inner cucumber-ness. "Sounds great."

Enough said. Right? Yeah, that was fine. She didn't want to

look overly enthusiastic. She'd save that for the in-bed portion of their evening.

Geez, she needed to get her mind out of the gutter. She'd gone from dinner and dancing to handcuffs and blindfolds in seconds. Oh, please let him be at least a little kinky.

"Ciara?"

"Yeah?" She blinked, still caught up in her fantasy sex life with Wesley.

"You feeling alright? You look a little flushed."

She'd be fine and dandy if she could get the real Wesley into her fantasy life. "Yep. Great. Go grab that champagne and get it on ice."

"You're the best, you know that, right?" Wes grabbed her in a bear hug and danced her around. He jerked back and rubbed at his chest. "Ouch, your necklace bit me."

"Oh, geez. Sorry." Ciara put her hand over the colorful pendant she'd gotten a few days ago. She didn't feel anything sharp.

"Pretty but painful, doll." Wes examined the charm, staring a scant inch above Ciara's boobs. "It would go with every-thing. Where'd you get it?"

Damn. She'd kind of hoped Wesley had sent it. Not likely, but she was ever hopeful. Must be from her mother, who rarely gave gifts. Weird.

"Oh my god, Ciara, there you are. I'm getting a divorce, or is it an annulment? Whatever. George is such an ass. I want out of this marriage right now." The bride ran into the kitchen and faux collapsed into Ciara's arms.

She glanced at Wes, who shook his head and smirked. He mouthed the words good luck and backed away from them.

This woman wasn't the first newlywed to freak out at the reception and she wouldn't be the last. Ciara had a long track-record of calming them down and helping them focus on what was important, their happily ever afters. Wesley called her the bride whisperer.

Ciara put a hand on the bride's arm and sent all the happy calming positive thoughts she could muster. They took a deep breath together.

"You can do this. Everything is going to be fine."

The bride nodded, looking a little dazed and repeated Ciara's words. "Everything is going to be fine."

A few hours later, the bride and groom had more than made up. The bouquet was tossed, the champagne chilled and toasted, the candles blown out, all topped off by the perfect sunset.

At two in the morning, Wes escorted the last of the drunken groomsmen to the limos they'd arranged to drive the non-sober home and Ciara collapsed into the nearest chair.

If she took her shoes off now, they were never ever going back on, but she'd limp home barefoot rather than take one more second in her not-so-high heels.

A lonely uneaten piece of wedding cake had been calling to her ever since she saw the fit groomsman walk away from it several hours ago. After that marathon wedding and reception, she needed a good sugar fix.

"Stop right there, thief." The deep rumble of a male voice halted the fork midway to her mouth. Sounded like he was back for his dessert. Oh God. How embarrassing.

"I'm just doing a bit of quality control. Have to make sure the cake is up to Willingham Weddings standards."

Please don't let him mention the fact that the wedding was over. Ciara turned to give the groomsman her best don't mind me I'm just the chubby, dateless, wedding planner stealing a piece of leftover cake smile. The man-slash-movie-star-slash-romance novel cover model standing three feet behind her had his arms crossed and a mad as hell glare on.

He wore a tight black t-shirt, dark jeans and a beautiful bright green crystal on a cord around his neck, so he wasn't the groomsman, or any other guest of the Ketcher-Fast wedding. She'd remember all that fantasy material.

He glanced down at the glowing charm at his throat and stilled. He faltered for a second and had to grab on to a chair to keep his balance.

Great. Another drunk guest and all the limos were gone. No way was she driving him home herself. Hmm. Well, maybe. He was awfully sexy and all those daydreams she'd had about Wes all night suddenly starred this magnetic stranger.

Until he growled at her. "I don't give a damn about the cake, unless that is where you've hidden my goods."

"Your goods?" The only goods Ciara could comprehend at the moment were six, or maybe eight, of the most beautifully defined abdominal muscles in the whole Four Corners.

He crossed the scant yard between them in two strides, hauled her up out of the chair, and got so far into her personal space bubble she could smell his cinnamony breath. A zing whipped through her from every place he touched and strangely, she really wanted to stand up on her tippy toes and press her lips to his, taste that spice, lick up every essence of that erotic flavor.

She might have too if he'd held her for a second longer. But, after searching her eyes, he released her and began pacing, prowling around her, his eyes roving her from head to toe.

He might have the body of a god and she the body of a cupcake, but she would not be intimidated by wandering eyes.

"First of all, you have to tell me what brand of toothpaste you use, and second, back up out of my business, buster."

"Do not try to beguile me with your talk of hygiene products, your hair of gold, and your body made for sin. Where have you hidden my Wyr relic, witch?" He stopped circling and stared straight at her butt.

Body made for sin? Was he kidding? Body made of sins, maybe. Namely the sins of Swiss meringue buttercream, chocolate ganache, and too many I Love Lucy reruns. "Stop staring at my tuchus. Whatever you're looking for ain't in there."

She wiggled her backside to emphasize her point. That made her intruder damn irritated, probably that her rear wasn't dropping any evidence of wrong doing based on the growl rumbling from his chest and his eyes glued to her ass.

"Stop enticing me with your curves, thief. You cannot distract me from what is mine."

Ciara cleared her throat, gently at first, but when that failed to bring his eyes up to hers, she about gave herself a sore throat trying to get his attention.

"Are you ill? I won't have you dying before you tell me where the statue is hidden."

What an asshat. A cute one, but a real douche canoe nonetheless. "I think maybe we've gotten off on the wrong foot here." Ciara extended her hand to him. "I'm Ciara Mosley-Willingham." Her hand hung there for a full count of ten. "And you are?"

He recoiled from her hand. "Wondering what kind of spell you're trying to work on me. Whatever it is, I assure you a Wyvern is immune."

"I was trying to be nice, but I've had a very long and tiring day, so my patience is wearing thin. I don't have your thingy, and I don't know what a why Vern is. I thought for a minute I might help you try to find it, but I'm done now." Ciara turned and began looking for her torturous heels. It would be much more fun to stomp off if there was some clack.

"As am I. If you won't return what you have taken from me I will be forced to bring you before the AllWyr council."

"What the hell?"

He grabbed her hand and pulled her through the ballroom toward a terrace. Good thing she'd already kicked off her shoes or she'd have been tripping all over her feet at the rate he was dragging her away.

"Hey, stop right this instant or I'll bring out the self-defense moves."

"Save your defense for the council. You'll need it."

This dude was seriously a wackadoo. Where was the pepper spray when she needed it? Oh, that's right, still in the bag from the store her mother had insisted they buy in bulk from.

"Let me go."

"Return my relic."

"I'm gonna make you a relic."

"Save your spells, witch."

"Your face is a witch."

The scary man released her and grabbed at his face. When he didn't find anything wrong with it, he narrowed his eyes and glared at her. "Good try, witch. You'll pay for that."

Ciara pivoted and bolted weaving her way between the tables. One second she was zigging and zagging, the next she was airborne.

Great talons gripped her shoulders and a deep whoosh-whoosh-whoosh sounded above her.

She wriggled and screamed, frantically trying to see what

was happening above her. Her feet crashed into empty glasses and caught a centerpiece of giant lilies dead-on as she was dragged through the air above the tables.

Before she could even take another breath to scream again, they swooped out of the French doors, over the balcony and into the night sky.

Ciara lost her effing mind as the ground beneath her sunk down into tiny squares of land. She couldn't look any longer, or she'd throw up. So instead she glanced up, not fathoming that she'd see flying above her the giant wings, flapping gracefully through the sky, of a dragon.

A WHOLE NEW WORLD

*T*he little thief wriggling in his talons was going to drive him batshit crazy.

No, no. She wasn't little. She was curvaceous, luscious. Absolutely edible. Good Gods, that ass. He could sink his hands into those hips and worship that plump rear end of hers for years, centuries, millennia. If she were anyone other than the thief who'd stolen the Wyr's most precious reliquary he'd wine and dine her, woo her with all his jewels and wealth until she agreed to go to bed with him.

As it were, if he didn't get her to reveal where she'd hidden the relic and how she'd stolen it in the first place, he'd have to take her before the AllWyr Council, and that meant admitting he'd lost the relic of the First Dragon.

There had to be another way to get her to talk.

"Let me go, you, you, monster."

You don't really want me to do that a hundred meters over the ocean do you, witch? That water is probably very cold and teeming with unfriendly sea life that would love to take a bite out of your plump ass.

"Eep." She stilled and fell silent. Whether it was his threat or because he'd spoken telepathically into her mind didn't matter. At least she wasn't wriggling below him anymore.

For seven blissful minutes they soared through the air toward the continent and his home. Cage Gylden's golden dragons waited for him every thousand kilometers or so into the flight and gave them another push with their power over the warm winds.

Surprisingly, he didn't need as much of their help coming back as he did going. He wasn't getting as tired, as if he had a renewed energy. He felt stronger now when he should already be exhausted.

The golds were discreet and kept well out of sight. He'd have a lot of explaining to do to Cage in the coming days about why he needed the emergency flight across the Atlantic on such short notice.

If he was lucky, he'd have the relic back before then.

"How did you do that?" The fear had gone from her voice. Interesting.

Do what?

"That. Talk but not talk. I can hear you in my head."

Silly witch. *I cannot speak in my dragon form.*

"No lips."

A chuckle rumbled through his chest. She was right.

"I hope that sound wasn't your stomach rumbling. Dragons don't eat people, right? You must eat sheep and small cows or something."

He'd love to eat her right up. *No dragons have eaten a human or a witch in several hundred years.*

"So, you aren't going to kill me?"

Not if you tell me where the reliquary is.

She fell silent again and he almost missed her prattling.

She had to be terrified flying through the air, across the middle of the ocean, in the night, in the talons of a dragon. There was a small glimmer of admiration that she wasn't acting the damsel in distress, one of those screaming Mimi scared women.

On the other claw, she'd stolen the First Dragon's heart. She deserved every misfortune he could inflict upon her body.

So, so many things he wanted to do to her body.

Another ten minutes and she was shivering enough that the rattle of her teeth worried him. He'd never get her to answer any questions if she froze to death. The warm air from the last gold dragon had faded too fast, and the sunrise was only just warming the sky.

He'd bring their altitude down but the coast was in sight and he didn't want to be spotted flying over France or Germany. *We're almost to my home.*

"Is that where you're taking me? Where exactly is your home or should I call it a lair? Oh God, do you live in a cave? Am I going to have to live amongst your giant piles of gold coins?"

Good to see hypothermia hadn't affected her ability to speak. He would begin his interrogation the second he got her inside. *I do not live in a cave. I have a villa in the countryside near Prague.*

"Really? I've always wanted to go to Prague."

This will be no vacation for you.

"Well, I'm certainly not recommending Dragon Airlines to my friends and family. The service sucks and the inflight food was horrible."

What a strange little witch he'd kidnapped. Jakob smiled to himself. Interrogation or not, he could hardly wait to see what she'd do next.

He'd get the relic back from her, no doubt, but he was going to have fun doing it.

A few moments later the Volga river came into view and he dropped to only a few hundred feet above the ground. His villa loomed in the distance. He could fly her directly to the second-floor guest room. He would stow her there behind locked doors until she revealed the relic, however, in the back garden stood a haystack for the animals from his summer wheat harvest.

Jakob circled the stack, getting lower with each pass and when they were a few meters above he opened his claws and dropped her directly on top.

She squealed and tumbled into the hay, getting buried in the stalks.

Bullseye.

He landed next to the stack and shifted back into his human form. The hay and area around them glowed with a green light. What the hell was going on with his soul shard? He tucked it into his shirt and called to his enchantress. "Ciara, my little witch, come out of your hiding place and tell me where you've hidden my relic."

"Ack." Rustling came from inside the haystack.

A light shined out from the stalks, matching that of his shard. Strange. But it guided him to her. "That is not a hiding place."

"Ooh. You shut up and get me out of here. I'm stuck. All I see are poky pieces of hay everywhere. It's a hay avalanche. I don't even know which way is up. Help."

Jakob reached one hand and arm in, rooted around for a minute and then grasped the shoulder he found. Too bad he hadn't accidentally come upon a softer part of her anatomy to grab on to. That beautiful heart-shaped ass for example.

Demons be damned, he couldn't get that particular part of her anatomy out of his head. It didn't matter one whit if her backside turned him all kinds of on or not. She was a witch and a thief and he would interrogate her to within a whisper of her life or until she gave back the relic.

He clasped the witch's shoulder tight and pulled her toward him until she popped out of the haystack tumbling head over tail, landing on top of him.

Her lush body pressed against him and he was instantly hard. It had to be a spell. No female, witch, fairy, demon, or human had ever addled his brain this way. Maybe she was a succubus.

"If you wanted a roll in the hay, all you had to do was buy me a drink and tell me I'm pretty. You didn't need to fly me halfway around the world."

For having been dragged halfway across the world, she was oddly calm. She brushed the hair off her face and sat up so that she was straddling him. Jesus, an inch lower and her sex would be perfectly aligned with his.

"Get off me."

A necklace with a crystal heart surrounded by wire shaped into quadrants representing the four elements dangled from her neck. It was almost as beautiful and fascinating as she was.

She picked another piece of hay out of her hair and straightened her clothes. "You get off me."

The tree in her necklace shimmered at him. "I'm not on you."

"Are you sure? I can't seem to move. You're doing something very mesmerizing with your eyes. It's making me want to lift up your shirt and sprinkle kisses all over your body."

Yes. She should do that, immediately.

"You are the one casting lust spells. I suggest you cease

immediately, they won't affect me and you'll only drain your energy. Now get off."

Jakob gripped her around the waist. Such a gorgeous, overfull hourglass figure she had. It took him a whole count of ten before he could talk himself into lifting her up and off instead of tighter to his own aching body.

He needed to get away from her before her spells took total control of his mind and made a liar out of him. In one fast movement he picked her up and stood, then stepped away.

"Hey. You're the one who kidnapped me, so don't go feeling all victimized that I landed on top of you. I'm sorry if I squished any manly bits."

"Manly bits?"

"Yes," she waved a hand below his belt, "you know, man parts, male anatomy, your penis. Wait, do dragon-men have penises?"

Jakob looked to where she indicated. "You were worried you damaged my cock?"

"Yes. I'm not exactly a lithe pixie if you hadn't noticed."

"I noticed." Boy, had he noticed. He couldn't stop noticing to the point where his tongue was ready to loll out of his head and drool all over her.

His witch's gaze went straight to the ground and she crossed one arm over the other. Her cheeks had gone a lovely blushed pink. He'd much rather see her skin flush from sexual pleasure than embarrassment. What in the world did she have to be embarrassed about?

Ah, she was human, and human culture had developed some bizarre fascination with half-dead twigs of women in the past hundred years. Ridiculous.

"Come along, luscious witch." He turned and strode

toward the French doors to his study that overlooked the gardens.

"I'm not going in your house. I don't know you, you could be a serial killer or a psycho or a—"

"Dragon?"

"If you'll just point me toward Prague, I'll be going now."

"It's a twelve hour walk to the outskirts of Prague from here. I don't think you'll make it without your shoes."

She looked down at her feet and wiggled her toes. He'd never really been one for a foot fetish, but she had sexy feet. Nails painted the exact shade of his iridescent green scales when he was in his dragon form.

"Come inside. I won't bite." Yet.

"Promise?"

"Of course." No.

He turned and walked toward the back terrace before he did bite her. Right in that sweet spot between her neck and shoulder. "We simply need to resolve this matter like adults."

She stayed put for another moment and then hurried to catch up with him. "Kidnapping me isn't exactly what I'd call a grown-up decision."

He shrugged, because it was either that or dip her over his arm and kiss his way across her chest. "You left me no choice."

"You could have believed me when I said I didn't have your thingamabob."

Why was she feigning this lack of knowledge about the relic? He could scent it on her. She must be a master at her craft, because he could also scent she wasn't lying, but he knew she was. "It's an ancient relic and you could have simply told me where it was, or even better given it back."

"But I don't have it."

Her truth, or her ignorance, or her spell smelled of a field after a fresh rain. "I can scent it on you."

"You've been smelling me?" She frowned. "That's weird."

"Dragons can scent treasure, emotions, desire." She smelled of all three. She wasn't scared, but she was interested. The underlying sweet musk of her arousal toward him was going to turn his brain to mush.

"Like a dog?"

"No. Quit stalling and come inside." He motioned toward the door holding out his arm hoping this time she would comply.

She straightened her spine, wrinkled up one side of her nose, and marched past him. Thank God.

He couldn't blame her for being cautious. In fact, he admired her courage. He had kidnapped her after all. She was being remarkably calm about the whole thing. Why was that?

They entered through his study and he led her through the grand room, intent on taking her to the antechamber of his trove. He'd be able to gauge her reaction, be able to watch for signs that she was nervous being there again. Maybe even get a tell on how she'd gotten in undetected.

But at the last moment, he veered toward the kitchen. "Are you hungry? It's midday, and I'm sure the cook has something delicious in the refrigerator or pantry." He kept his tone light and inviting. Maybe if she felt welcome and relaxed instead of kidnapped and persecuted she would simply give him the relic back.

"Umm. I'm good. Thanks though."

"Perhaps some wine then. Our local Moravian vintages are quite nice."

"Why are you being so nice to me all of a sudden?"

Busted.

"I told you, we can settle this like adults. We'll eat, drink, and you'll tell me where you've hidden the relic."

"But I honestly don't know what you're talking about."

She must have cast a spell that cloaked her lies. He should be able to scent them. No one could lie to a dragon, however, she clearly was.

"Fine. We'll do it your way." Enough was enough. Jakob grabbed the witch by the wrist and dragged her back into the great room and then up the stairs.

"Where are we going? Stop. Let go. You're hurting me."

He slammed open the door to the guest room, with its four-poster bed where he could tie her up and torture her until she came…uh, told him what she'd done with the relic.

"No, no, no." The witch tried to stop and pull away from him, fighting to get out of his grasp.

She was no match for him. He continued into the room and threw her on the bed.

"Get away from me. I will scream. Surely someone will stop you from hurting me." She scrambled off and held out her hands, glaring at him.

So fierce. So fucking gorgeous.

"I have never and would never brutalize a woman. But I am not above intense interrogation. Tell me where the relic is and we can avoid all of this."

"I don't have your god-damned relic, you dickwad," she yelled, and a white wind blew her hair.

Her anger zipped around them, stinging his senses. She was finally losing her Zen-like cool. Now he was getting somewhere.

He'd push her until she let her delicious powers loose. He could practically taste the flavor of her intense emotions that lay beneath the surface. "Then who does?"

"How am I supposed to know, you fucktard?" The humidity was sucked out of the room and tiny snowflakes crystalized around her.

Interesting mix of powers. Did she control wind and temperature? She'd be the perfect match for a golden dragon.

The bottom of his stomach opened into a black abyss at the thought of any other dragon possessing her. More of her spells no doubt.

He was on a roll, pushing her. Soon her cloak would break and he'd pinpoint her lies. "Do you have a partner? Tell me, did your coven help you steal it?"

"I don't have a coven, because I'm not a witch, asshat."

Her name-calling was beginning to amuse him. He needed to stay angry. Retrieving the relic was more important than his damned attraction to her.

The shard hiding beneath his shirt buzzed as if it didn't agree.

"If you're not a witch, why were you casting spells?"

She punched the bed, then looked at her fist, her pretty blue eyes wide and for the first time, scared. She took a deep breath, closed her eyes, and took another. When she opened them again, the wind along with the frost in the air, as well as her fear and anger were gone.

Too bad. She was damn sexy when she was all worked up.

In a tone he could only call dulcet, she said, "I am not a witch. I am a wedding planner. I do not know what a relic is or where yours might be. I did not steal anything from you. Now please take me home."

Wasn't that interesting. She'd gone from emotions so strong her magic manifested around her, to calm and collected, magic banked away, in the matter of two breaths.

That was not a skill she'd come up with in the last minute. This was practiced.

Who or what in her life troubled her so badly that she'd had to learn to hide her true emotions this way?

A flight across the ocean in his dragon form hadn't scared her enough to make her subservient to his wishes. Plying her with kindness hadn't worked. Demanding the information and raising her ire had gotten him closer.

Emotions would be the key to breaking her, but anger wouldn't work. She'd proven her ability to mask and control that. He would need to develop a completely different plan of attack to get what he wanted from her.

Anger and hate were strong emotions. So was lust.

He already knew she was attracted to him. She hadn't been able to hide that.

If she wouldn't tell him what he wanted to know, he'd seduce it out of her.

In bed.

With her moaning under him.

Moaning his name.

Only his name.

DRAGON'S LAIR

*C*iara called upon every yoga class and meditation she'd ever done in her life to calm herself and not strangle the bejeesus out of this guy. Dragon...guy.

For a minute, she'd let her emotions get the better of her. She knew better than that. Emotional outbursts were for sissies and were not tolerated in her home. Rather her mother's home.

No one got to her. Not anymore.

In a matter of minutes, this man-dragon or whatever he was had taken her through a gambit of emotions from fear to lust to anger to lust and back again.

Enough of that.

Ciara had never met a person she couldn't calm down and get to see a dire situation in a new light. It was her greatest skill. The only way she could do that was to remain calm herself.

But this guy wasn't a guy at all. Was he even a human? Would sensible talk work on a shape-shifting dragon? She'd have to up her game to get him to see her way and let her go.

He was being completely unreasonable about the whole relic thing. That was an emotional trigger point for him. Talking to him about that wasn't going to get her anywhere.

What he had responded to was her accidental flirting. Some of the things that had come out of her mouth tonight, whew. If she could only talk like that to Wes, they'd be married and on a permanent honeymoon.

Lust was the right emotion, but she sucked at flirting on purpose. It was weird and awkward every time. She got too far inside her own head wondering if the guy was thinking she sounded completely ridiculous.

She felt ridiculous trying to come on to men most of the time. Sure, they all wanted a good roll in the hay, but with a chubby girl like her?

She and the dragon man had already rolled in the hay. Literally. He seemed to like it. Okay then, she'd channel her inner Marilyn Monroe and Happy Birthday, Mr. President him.

God, she was going to look absurd.

Ciara licked her lips and his eyes went straight to her mouth. Sweet. That gave her the confidence boost she needed to do this seduction thing. She took a step closer and straightened her back, hoping her boobs would continue the distraction.

"What are you doing, witch?" His voice was a low purr, not a question.

"Please, call me Ciara." She walked right into his personal space and placed a finger on his shirt, fiddling with his button. "I don't even know your name."

She said it in her best breathy voice, which she didn't even have to fake.

He didn't step away or remove her hand. That was a good

sign. "I am Jakob Zeleny, Wyvern of the Green Dragon warriors."

There was that word again. Did it mean leader? "Sounds important."

She walked her fingers further up his shirt. She was so close to touching his skin she could almost taste it. This was the worst plan ever. Warmth filled the room, swirling around them.

The fireplace on the other wall burst to life filling the space with light and heat. Uh, automatic timer?

"I've never met a witch who had command of more than one element. Is that why you stole the relic? You think it will give you power over earth as well?"

If she played along with this witchcraft baloney, maybe she'd learn something to help her get out of this situation. "What would I do with power over earth? Make mud pies?"

"Or mud baths." His voice had dropped making that statement sound like a very naughty invitation.

The skin she was so close to touching smelled of earth. Not in grimy way, but like a fresh field newly sown, where green things could grow. Which was a really strange thought for her. She was a city girl. The only fields she'd ever seen were on TV, at golf courses, or around event centers.

What was her brain doing thinking about what he smelled like anyway? She needed to focus on getting the hell out of here. Not on if that spot right below his chin would taste as delicious as she thought it would.

No, no, no. Mind, out of gutter, now. Back to the work at hand.

"Mud baths, huh? Sounds dirty." Whoops. Her voice had gone all husky and her fingers had walked their way up his shirt to the open button.

"Mmm-hmm." He rumbled. Lust laced every syllable he spoke. "I'd love to see you naked and covered in mud."

This guy was a sicko, or she was, because she was completely turned on by the idea of rolling around naked in the mud with him.

"Well, maybe we can do that after you take me home." What was she saying? At least she'd gotten half of it right with the taking her home part. God, she must have Stockholm Syndrome already. She was having a hard time concentrating on her plan to seduce him into doing what she wanted, while standing this close to him and feeling the heat pouring off of his body. Being kidnapped and held hostage was not supposed to make her want to strip her assailant of all of his clothes and lick him from nose to toes.

He ran the backs of his knuckles across her shoulder and down her arm, creating a trail of goosebumps that sprang up in his wake. His hand slipped off of her elbow and continued down to land on her waist.

Whoo boy. She would not acknowledge the tingles that sent down her spine and between her legs.

"I'll be happy to take you home as soon as you return the relic." He made that sound like the best idea ever. She almost wished she had his stupid relic, just so she could give it to him and then have her way with him.

She was trying to avoid the topic of the damn thing, and normally it was a piece of pie to keep anyone away from whatever had them agitated.

The problem was, he had her completely worked up. God, she hoped she was having at least the same effect on him. Probably not. Time to take it up another notch.

"I can think of so many more fun things for us to do than argue." Like that mud bath he'd mentioned.

The hand at her waist snaked along to her back and hugged her to him so that she could feel every bit of him against every bit of her. Unless that was a relic in his pocket, there was a whole lot of him that her girly bits would sure like to get to know.

"Yes, luscious witch, why don't we see where this can go?" He stared down into her eyes and the sparkle he dazzled her with kept her from noticing that he was slowly backing her toward the bed until her butt hit the footboard.

Now wait just a damn minute. Just who was seducing whom here?

Her hand, fully of its own accord, went up and touched his cheek. The scruff there that scratched against her hand would feel even better between her legs. He was so damn good-looking. Even more handsome than Wesley.

At least Wes was actually attracted to her. Probably. This guy, she doubted if he truly wanted her at all. He just wanted the thing she had supposedly stolen from him. So, what the hell was she doing right now?

She needed a new plan. Because this one was definitely not working.

Plan A was getting her into more trouble.

Plan B would have a whole lot more of her getting the hell out of here.

She would lie her way out of this. Convince him she would do what he wanted and simply get him to return her. Yeah.

"Why don't you show me to a phone, so I can call home and have them retrieve your relic." Her voice would sound a whole lot calmer, like she wanted it to, if her breathing wasn't so rapid and her heart wasn't going kaboom kaboom kaboom.

Those sexy sleepy eyes of Jakob's sparkled. "A thief, and now a liar too."

Dammit. She knew she was a crappy liar. But he wasn't supposed to know that. "I'm neither."

Her tone was a little less offended than she'd tried to make it.

"Remember I told you dragons can scent emotions. That includes desire and lies. Your defenses are weakening. Or that's the first lie you've told me."

There went Plan B to shit.

"It is not. I lied when I said a mud bath sounded like fun."

He chuckled. "You never said that. But I like that you thought it, and you were turned on by that thought."

Wait, did he say he could smell desire? She would be a liar if she tried to tell herself she hadn't felt any of that for him.

She didn't desire this man, she wanted Wesley Alexander. Yeah, dammit.

Jakob's head tilted slightly to the side and he raised an eyebrow. "What kind of scheme are you cooking up in that pretty little head of yours? The scent of deceit is pouring out of you."

"I... I... I'm not cooking up anything except how the hell to get out of here and away from you." She put her hands against his chest and pushed. He didn't move even a little bit.

"That delicious musky flavor coming from your sex says otherwise." He lowered his head and brushed his lips ever so gently across hers.

She should bite him, she should kick and scream, she shouldn't open her mouth and whimper, wanting so much more.

"Mmm." His tongue dipped into her mouth teasing her. "You may smell like lies, but you taste of chocolate and champagne."

He mumbled the words against her, sending all kinds of tingles across her lips.

"Cake." Her tongue darted out, trying to entice him. This one little kiss was the most action she'd gotten in months. Okay, that was another lie that he could probably smell, because it had been years.

Had she forgotten how good kisses were? Because this was the simplest kiss, sweet and innocent, and she was ready to melt into a puddle on the floor.

"Cake?" He said the word, and then tasted her again.

"Chocolate wedding cake." All wedding cake should be chocolate, especially if it had a guy like this enjoying the taste of her.

This was exactly what she'd imagined her first kiss with Wes would be like. Kind of. Her fantasies were quite a bit dirtier than this. Jakob's hold on her waist was possessive, but his kiss was not. This position she'd gotten herself into meant he could pretty much do as he liked at the moment.

But he wasn't doing anything more than tempting her.

He nibbled at the corner of her mouth and it dawned on her that he was waiting for her permission, for her to tell him that this was what she wanted.

What a strange thing for a kidnapper to do.

What a strange thing for a kidnappee to want.

She did want it, and him. That was some long-buried emotion and unfulfilled needs talking. They needed to shut the hell up. They didn't get to talk.

"Jakob, stop."

He froze, mid nibble.

"We hardly know each other, and besides I have a boyfriend." That was only a partial lie, hardly even a white one, because she did have a date and that was halfway to boyfriend.

Jakob stiffened, released her, and stepped away. "Ah, I see."

He did? "Oh, good. So, no more kissing or…"

If he hadn't smelled that lie, it must be true. Yeah, keep telling yourself that, Ciara.

"No, that is your choice. You may choose torture instead of seduction." Jakob crossed the room and yanked the door open.

"Torture?" Was that her voice that squeaked like that?

"Yes, witch." Every other time he'd called her a witch, it hadn't sounded like an insult. "I had thought to seduce the relic from you. But if you prefer lies over my kisses, you may have it that way."

"Hey, I was the one seducing you." She meant to shout that, girl power style. Unfortunately, that squeak in her voice was still there.

"I suggest you think long and hard about telling me exactly where you and your cohorts have hidden the relic. We'll pick this up again in this evening." He walked out the door, shut it behind him, and Ciara heard the click of a lock.

She ran across the room and yanked on the door handle, then pounded against the door. "You don't have to get all butt hurt, just because I think you're a cruddy kisser." Hopefully the big wooden door between them would block the scent of that little fib.

Ciara glanced around the room looking for any other way out. There were two large windows on either side of the bed, and even if she did have to wait until evening it wouldn't be long. The sun was already sinking into late afternoon, even though it felt like morning to her.

She refused to be a damsel in distress. There had to be a way out of here. She slid one of the windows up and immediately talked herself out of trying to jump down. She'd break both of her legs, maybe a hip, probably a couple ribs, her arm, and her neck if she tried to jump from here.

The bed in the room was at least a king, which meant really big sheets. Did that thing people did in the movies where they tied sheets together and climbed out of the window actually work? She was going to find out or die trying. Hopefully not the die trying part.

She threw back the covers and yanked at the top sheet. Geez, these had to be 5000 thread count.

She was kind of tired. Jet-lag or dragon-lag, which ever. The time change and no sleep was taking its toll on her. Maybe just a little nap before she tried to escape.

A quiet knock sounded at the door. Maybe her dumbass dragon had come back to apologize. Or maybe he'd come back to torture her like he promised. She picked up the lamp from the bedside table and held it like a baseball bat. The door creaked open and a plump older woman stuck her face into the room.

"Dobry den. I am Mrs. Bohacek. Jakob asked me to come up and make sure you were comfortable."

"He did? Wait, are you a dragon too?" Ciara hefted the lamp slightly higher. Not that she could actually knock this adorable grandmother across the head with it, but grandma didn't need to know that.

"Ha. No, kiddo. I'm not." She walked into the room carrying a tray with a mug and some sort of cookies on it in one hand, and had green flowing material draped over the other arm. She kicked the door shut with her foot, ruining any plan Ciara might have had to run out.

"Then what are you?" Ciara wasn't quite ready to set down her baseball bat lamp weapon yet.

Mrs. Bohacek crossed the room and set the fabric on the bed and the tray with the snack on the table. "I'm a lot of things. A little bit nanny, a goddess, a little bit witch." She held out her hand for the lamp and Ciara handed it over.

She was never going to use it anyway. "You're a witch?"

"I am, just the same as you." Mrs. Bohacek returned the lamp to its place on the bedside table, then held out the green material, which turned out to be a dress, to Ciara.

"I'm a nice person, really." Ciara took the dress from her and found it insanely soft to the touch.

"Most witches are. I've only ever known one that I didn't get along with, but whoever really gets along with their siblings? Rivalry and all that, you know."

"I don't understand why you to think I'm a witch. If I had magical powers, it would make my job a heck of a lot easier."

"Doesn't it?"

"I can't make things fly across the room or magically appear." She could think of at least half a dozen flakey grooms that she would have liked to make magically disappear though.

Mrs. Bohacek twirled her fingers indicating that Ciara should turn around, so she could undo the zipper on the formal gown she had on. The dress that Mrs. Bohacek brought did look a hell of a lot more comfortable than the suck-you-in-until-you-can't-breath shapewear she had on.

"That's the kind of magic in the movies. Mine and yours is something much more... useful."

Ciara breathed a sigh of relief as the zipper came down on her gown. Before she could even feel weird about getting undressed in front of this woman, she was out of her uncomfortable undergarments and into the softest dress in the universe. What in the world was this thing made out of?

She felt more like she was wearing pajamas than a pretty frock.

"It's part of why Jakob is so attracted to you." Mrs. Bohacek picked up the clothes from the floor, folded them, and set them on a chair.

"He's not attracted to me. He thinks I'm a thief and a liar."

The fire in the fireplace snapped, crackled, and threw sparks out into the room, singeing the carpet.

Ciara watched wide-eyed as Mrs. Bohacek flicked her wrist and put out the flames with the tiniest of rainstorms, then swished her hand again and a hot wind dried the carpet.

"Tomorrow, maybe we will have some time to help you get those emotions –"

"Under control." That was the same line her mother had been railing at her for years. But, she hadn't had some sort of an outburst, or cried, or even frowned for that matter.

"I was going to say out. Keep suppressing them the way you have been, and you'll burn the whole villa down. Your magic is more powerful around Jakob."

Was she inferring that the fire had something to do with Ciara's emotions? This was all way too weird and wasn't getting her any closer to escaping.

"Never mind." Back to the escape plan. Ciara hoped the connection she already felt with this woman would work to her advantage. "Mrs. Bohacek, I really need to get out of here. I need to get home."

"You don't want to do that."

"I do though. I really, really do."

Mrs. Bohacek muttered something under her breath which Ciara only caught part of. Something about all they'd done to get these two together. She shrugged and tipped her head to the side. "It might be fun to see Jakob chase his mate across the countryside. As long as he doesn't take too long about claiming you."

What the heck was this beautiful grandma lady talking about? "I don't understand what you're talking about."

Mrs. Bohacek crossed the room and opened the door, waiting for Ciara to follow her. Awesome. She was going to help.

Ciara tiptoed down the stairs across a cold tiled hallway and into a warm and inviting kitchen. This must be the back door. Damn, she didn't see any way out from here. The only door Mrs. Bohacek opened was the refrigerator. She got out a butter dish and a jar of jelly and set them on the counter. Then she grabbed a loaf of bread and proceeded to make toast. "Would you like a cup of coffee? Or maybe hot tea if you're going sleep tonight?"

Mrs. Bohacek stared at Ciara then grabbed some K cups out of a drawer along with two mugs. "Coffee it is then."

"Are you going to help me get out of here or not?"

"Or not. It can be dangerous around here in the dark, which isn't too far off. Besides, I want to see my Jakob and you happily mated."

Mated. That was a weird phrase for her to keep using. Happily married, Ciara understood. While Mrs. Bohacek's English was perfect, they were in a Slavic country, so maybe something was getting lost in translation.

"I don't intend on marrying anyone I have just met and especially not someone who has kidnapped me."

"Marriage is a whole other step. Mated is what I said. You're Jakob's true mate."

DOWN TO THE DUNGEON

*J*akob was this close to shifting back into his dragon form, ripping the French doors off his office and digging a giant hole smack dab in the middle of his wild-style garden. Which was something he hadn't done in a good hundred years. Not since he was a youngling and had been yelled at by his father for trying to impress one of the villager girls with his wings.

What he wouldn't give to be able to ask his father's advice on what to do with the woman upstairs. But his father was gone, and he was the one who people came to for advice now that he was the Green Dragon Wyvern.

He sank back into his office chair and inhaled the scent of the myriad of green and flowering plants around him. The office may look more like a jungle than the spartan rooms his father kept, but he was half the age his father had been when he became Wyvern. Jakob knew he could draw strength and focus from having as much of mother nature inside as he had outside. He drew his power from the earth, could manipulate it, and use the ground, trees, and growing things to his advantage.

He ought to fill the guest room upstairs with every potted plant in the place, so he wouldn't strangle the curvy witch up there. Because she was most definitely driving him crazy. It was either strangle her or fuck her silly.

They both needed time to cool down. He'd leave her up there for a few more hours before attempting to interrogate her again.

He had hoped to already have the First Dragon's relic back in his possession by now. He had precious little time before he would need to reveal the theft to the other Wyverns.

Match would be coming by in the next few days to check on how Jakob was settling into being the Green Wyvern.

He really didn't want the loss of the dragon's most important sacred item to be the first thing that people thought of when they remembered Jakob's rule.

Match was the first of their generation to inherit his Wyr and had assumed the role all Red Wyverns did. First son of the first son. Alpha among alphas.

If you asked Jakob, Match was a cranky old bastard, who acted more like he was pushing six centuries rather than a bit over two-hundred years.

He would give Jakob hell the minute he realized the First Dragon's relic wasn't exactly where it was supposed to be—entrusted to the green dragons and hidden away deep underground.

How the hell had Ciara even gotten into his lair? It had every state-of-the-art security system, plus every ward and magical deterrent available to him. He didn't have time to investigate his lair's protection shortcomings and get the relic back from Ciara. He hated to have anyone else in, around, or near his treasure, but he hated the thought of having another dragon in, around, or near, especially not in, his little thief.

There were few dragons he trusted enough to even know where his lair and treasures lie. He and Steele had done much of their warrior training together and battled many a demon dragon at each other's backs these past years. Steele was still young for a dragon warrior, not even in his prime yet. Although Jakob was only a few years older.

Match had questioned Jakob when he chose Steele to be his second. Cage and Ky had backed him. Even if they hadn't, Jakob knew who he could count on.

Jakob pulled his mobile phone from his pocket and sent a quick text to Steele to find out how quickly he could get to the villa. Steele replied right away and would be there within an hour.

Patience was not his best virtue. Luckily, he had a mountain of paperwork to keep him occupied. He signed a few invoices, wondered what Ciara was doing, read a dispute he needed to mediate between a green and a red dragon, pictured Ciara naked in his head, and growled at his own hard on.

It had to be simply because there was a lush ripe woman in his house. It had nothing to do with her beguiling smile, her pure sensuality, or the way her hips swayed when she walked. Of course not.

He had been without a woman for too long. That was all. He'd been under a thousand skirts in the past fifty years, but not even one since he'd become Wyvern. He'd been too busy. His cock had chosen today to protest that fact.

Fine. He'd go to Prague the next chance he had and wine and dine the pants off the first woman he met.

Except the idea didn't excite him at all. Not like the

woman upstairs did anyway.

Steele sauntered into Jakob's office a few minutes later. Jakob decided to stay in the chair behind his desk rather than try to hide or ignore the tent in his pants. Getting his mind back on the problem at hand would help it go away faster than anything else.

"What's up, boss?" Steele plopped down into a chair on the other side of the desk.

Jakob steepled his fingers and said, "My lair has been broken into."

Steele's easy pose straightened, and he sat up. "Holy shit. How could that even happen?"

"I don't know, but you're going to find out for me," Jakob growled.

Steele's eyes widened but he stayed silent.

"I've already caught the thief. If she reveals anything, I'll let you know."

"She?" Was there some insinuation in Steele's tone? Probably. He was a smart dragon with keen senses.

"Yes, the thief is a witch. A powerful one. My best guess is she is trying to gain power over the earth element."

The tattoo at Steele's neck writhed. No green dragon would take that news lightly. "What's her element now?"

Ciara had denied knowledge of her powers, but her passion had given her away. As soon as he could, Jakob was going to tap into that. "That's the interesting part. I saw her control wind and fire."

Steele whistled.

Yes, Jakob's sweet witch and her power was that impressive.

"Where did you find her?"

"The Atlantic Coast of the United States." There weren't

any green dragons living in that area, which was why Jakob decided to follow the trail the relic had left all the way across the damned ocean. "What kind of contacts do we have in that area?"

Steele thought for a minute. "I did a few training exercises with a red dragon named Dax last year. He's stationed over there somewhere."

Jakob knew Steele well enough to understand that training exercises was code for late nights at the strip club. God, how he missed those days.

"Good. Coordinate with the Golds to get over there. I'll assign Merc to your post in Switzerland for the time being."

"Will do." Steele shoved out of his chair and headed for the door. "Hey, glad to see you finally found yourself a companion."

Jakob frowned. "I'm not that far into my prime that I need to settle down."

His sex life had been sorely lacking, but he was not a fuddy duddy like Match. Yet.

"Then who is the sex on a stick in the kitchen making toast? I smell her all over you."

The dragon part of Jakob bristled, pushing its way to the surface. A ripple of green scales passed over his skin. His dragon was more on edge about the obvious appreciation of Ciara in Steele's voice than the fact that she had apparently escaped from her room.

"You get to America and worry about her coven. I'll take care of the witch in the kitchen."

"Give me a week's leave when this is over, and I won't tell anyone you're a softy when it comes to jailing pretty women."

"Get out." Jakob pointed to the French doors and Steele

laughed and pushed his way out the doors. He shifted to his dragon form and took flight almost instantly.

Jakob headed toward the kitchen, making sure to walk silently so as to surprise his escaped prisoner. Less than a meter from the doorway, he heard her talking and then growl in frustration.

"I am not admitting to liking Jakob even a little bit."

Was she talking to herself or the toast? Because he, Steele, and Ciara were the only ones in the villa today. He'd sent everyone else away when he first discovered the theft. None of his human staff would dare steal from him, and he would have been able to smell it on any of them. Besides, they were all very loyal with most having served their whole lives for either him or his father.

Once he'd dismissed them, the scent of the thief had practically overwhelmed his senses. She smelled of sunshine and licorice.

He would never get enough of that scent.

When he poked his head around the door, he saw no one else in the kitchen besides her. It was pretty damn cute that she was trying to convince herself she wasn't attracted to him.

"You don't have to admit to it. I know how much you want me."

Ciara spun around and threw her piece of toast at him. He dodged it easily and they both watched it land jelly side up.

That had to be one of her more useful spells.

"You scared the pee out of me."

Ciara stood before him, her hands on her hips, and those hips, and thighs, and breasts, were covered in the deepest of green silk. The material hugged all of her curves in the best way. That hard on he'd successfully managed to subdue popped right back up. First Dragon help him, she was so damned gorgeous.

If she were anyone but a relic stealing thief he'd already have her splayed out on the counter, legs spread wide, with his head between them.

He'd bet her pussy tasted better than any dessert.

Unfortunately he would never get to find out because Wyr business was more important than his dick. He'd have to find an old sack for her to wear because if he was going to keep his head in the game, he wouldn't be able to do it with her wearing a dress the exact color of his scales. She was a sly one to use that trick to mess with his mind.

"How did you get out of your jail cell? I had planned on only bread and water for you until you reveal the location of the relic."

"Mrs. Bohacek helped me... uh, find the kitchen." Ciara indicated toward the toaster, then frowned and shook her head. "Where did she go?"

Jakob didn't know anyone by that name. She was clearly trying to distract him from his own question. "Good try."

"No, seriously?" Ciara spun in a slow circle searching the kitchen.

"Enough." He grabbed her by the arm, careful not to hold her so tightly that she would bruise, and dragged her from the room.

"Where are you taking me now?"

He pulled her toward the stairs but veered to the side. He shoved aside a potted plant on a small table in the corner. Behind it, hidden well among the decorative wainscoting on the wall, was a rectangular piece of plastic that looked like an ordinary outlet. Jakob pressed and a fingerprint scanner popped out. He swiped his thumb and the wall slid open.

"Whoa." She stopped tugging to get out of his grip and stared into the secret passage.

"Come. I want you to show me exactly how you got in and out of here with the relic." Before she could protest, he pulled her in and the door shut behind them. His eyes flickered, and his dragon sight allowed him to see perfectly well with ambient light coming from his soul shard.

Not something it normally did, until yesterday.

"I can't even see my hand in front of my face."

Jakob tapped a panel and small lights blinked on, illuminating the long spiral staircase in front of them.

"Oh man. This is the part where you lock me in your dungeon, never to see the light of day again, isn't it?"

"That all depends on you." For the first time since he'd taken her yesterday, he caught a whiff of fear from her. Good. Maybe they'd actually get somewhere now. And after they did, he'd be sure she was never frightened by anyone or anything ever again.

Not that her well-being was his job.

Instead of guiding her down the staircase he grabbed her around the waist and jumped over the side of the railing with her. She screamed and clung to him, which he enjoyed immensely. A small spark of the magic he'd been given the day he got his soul shard, pushed out and he unfurled his dragon wings. They caught on the rush of air and helped him to glide the ten or so meters to the cavern floor.

When they landed, she still had her face buried in his chest. His wings, of their own accord, curled forward and wrapped around them both, hugging her tighter to him. He stroked her hair. "You're all right now."

She didn't move, so he lifted her chin with one knuckle. Her eyes were screwed shut. "Ciara. You can open your eyes."

One eye peeked out at him, then shut again. The sensation of a fiery heat coupled with an icy chill rushed over his skin. Ciara opened both eyes and stared up at him.

"You. Are. An. Asshat."

"I think you called me that one already." Jakob pulled his wings back and pushed the partial shift back down. He released his hold on her, before he did something stupid like try to kiss her again.

Her scent was even more intoxicating underground than it had been in the villa. Maybe it had been a mistake to bring her down here. He turned and walked down the hallway that was half modern construction and half carved out of the earth and stone. It took a few moments for her to follow, but as soon the staircase lights blinked off, she squeaked and caught up to him.

They descended along a gently sloping incline that twisted its way deeper into the earth. The farther they went, the more primitive the tunnel became, until the only modern-day electronics remaining were the secondary fingerprint scanner and retinal scan terminal at the locked double doors to his lair.

They were almost fifty meters underground now, and the scent of her was so strong that it was as if he was already inside of her.

This had definitely been a mistake. He quickly swiped his finger and aligned his face for the scanner. The door whooshed open. Now he would see how Ciara reacted to being back at the scene of the crime.

She stepped into the cavern and stared around with her jaw open. She looked like a kid who had never even tasted a lollipop, standing at the entrance to the world's largest candy store. Except this wasn't candy. It was gold, and art, and rare books, and the largest collection of heirloom seeds in the world. And she wasn't a kid, she was a thief.

"You think I took something from this place?"

"I tire of your denial, Ciara."

"You said you can smell lies. Take a good sniff, then tell me again that I'm lying."

Fire danced in her eyes and across his skin. The scent of her fear was gone, and it had been replaced, not by deceit, but desire. Nothing this far underground had seen the sun in hundreds of years, but the scent of sunshine on a warm spring day surrounded him.

She wasn't lying. Yet along with her natural perfume, he could not only scent the relic, but he could even feel its power on her. Here, where it had been kept for the past 700 years, its magic—the same each soul shard a dragon warrior wore—flowed in and around both of them.

The little stone in the necklace she had on lit up with a green light that matched the incessant glow from his soul shard. It was as if she had her own shard.

But that couldn't be. Only dragons were given a shard of the First Dragon's soul, and it imbued them with the power to shift. There were no such thing as female dragons. Only sons of sons of sons of the First Dragon.

If he could touch the necklace, hold it in his hand, maybe then he could understand. "I believe you. There are a lot of unanswered questions though."

"Finally. So, can I go home now? I've got a lot to do, not to mention my date on Wednesday."

Jakob rankled at the mention of a date. She wouldn't be going on any dates with anyone, except maybe him. "Where did you get that necklace?"

Ciara touched her neck and seem surprised that the charm

was glowing. "Someone gave it to me as a present. I just don't know who. My mother, I suppose. However, that is very atypical for her."

The air around them frosted, but not in the pleasurable tingly way it had before. Icicles formed on the wall nearest them. Ciara wrinkled her nose. "Oops."

"Oops?"

"Yes, your Mrs. Bohacek told me I needed to not suppress my emotions while I was here because I might burn the house down. I guess icicles are better than flames."

There was a new vulnerability in her voice.

One that Jakob wanted to hear more of.

It was really too bad that dragons didn't have mates anymore and hadn't for almost seven-hundred years, because he could sure imagine himself with Ciara for a good long time. Maybe Steele was right, and he did need a companion. But that term didn't seem right for Ciara at all.

What did seem right was to do something no one since his grandfather's generation had. Right now, standing with her amongst all of his treasure, what he wanted more than anything else was to lick his way across her shoulder and bite into that soft, supple flesh, claiming her.

Ridiculous.

He might do it anyway.

"Ciara, come here my little witch." What would she taste like? He needed to know.

"What? I'm sorry about the icicles. They'll melt, won't they?"

"I don't care about the ice, although I do like the fire."

His fingers hovered above her arm, ready to pull her to him.

A shrill alarm blasted through the air, and the door to the vault flashed with lights that indicated it would shut soon.

Shit.

That alarm only meant one thing.

Demon dragons.

"Do not move from this spot." Jakob pointed at Ciara. "You will be safe here."

He bolted for the door, already letting the shift take over, claws and talons sprouting, his wings unfurling.

"Hey, where are you going? What am I supposed to do?" Ciara scrambled to follow him.

Jakob used his power over the earth to put up a wall of rocks between her and the door.

You can think about all the trouble you've caused.

"If you think I've caused trouble, you haven't seen anything yet," she shouted before the door slammed shut.

Jakob flew through the tunnel moving the earth out of his way as fast as he could. Instead of flying up the stairwell he carved a new path straight up into the grounds of the Villa. Dusk had only just settled, but a half dozen demon dragons slinked out of the shadows.

Trouble indeed.

WHOA, OH, IT'S MAGIC

*U*m, what?

He could not be serious. Stay here? Think about the trouble she'd caused?

Blow me.

As soon as Ciara shook off the shock of Jakob locking her in his treasure trove, she started looking for a way out. The space-aged doors seemed locked up pretty damn tight, but there had to be a release mechanism from the inside.

She found a keypad set into the rock wall next to the metal doors, but there weren't any numbers or letters to enter a password. Not that she'd have any idea what the code could be.

Probably asshat69 or ImSexyAF.

Waving her arms around, pounding on the door, and trying to pry it open with her fingernails didn't work. Kicking it only hurt her bare big toe.

Finally, the blaring alarms quit and she could hear herself think again.

This place was huge. There had to be a backdoor.

She climbed over a pile of gold coins feeling a whole lot like Scrooge McDuck. How cliché was he to keep mountains of jewels and gold bars laying around? If she didn't want to get away from him so badly, she'd take a little something just to irritate the hoarder.

Behind a shelf filled with framed paintings of women in various states of undress, all by artists long dead, a small two-seat café table and chairs sat. It wasn't an antique or anything and sitting smack dab in the middle was a tiered tray with finger sandwiches, scones, petit fours, and jammy thumbprint cookies. There were even two teacup and saucers.

Who in the hells bells was having a tea party in the middle of a dragon's lair?

Mrs. Bohacek appeared from the opposite direction wearing a beautiful flowing white dress and carrying a tray with a steaming pot of something spicy and fragrant, a small creamer jug, and tiny ramekins of sliced lemons and sugar cubes.

"The tea is a cinnamon rooibos. Would you like cream or lemon in yours?" she said and set the tray on the table.

Aha. So there was another entrance to the cavern.

"Thanks, but no thanks. If you'll just point me in the direction of the exit, I'd like to get the heck out of here and back to my life."

"Yes, yes." She waved Ciara to the other seat at the table and sat down. She poured them both a cup of the delicious smelling tea. "But first let's have a little snack to fortify ourselves. Magic is taxing work, you know."

No, she didn't know. She wasn't going to have high tea either. Dammit.

A flash of anger she couldn't suppress bubbled up and out before she even recognized she'd lost control of her emotions.

Mrs. Bohacek pulled the cup she'd been sipping on from her lips and tipped it upside down. Nothing came out. She gave it a shake and a large round tea-colored ice cube fell to the table.

"Better ice than fire, I guess. I warned you about trying to quash those emotions of yours, but I appreciate that you didn't boil my tea and burn my mouth."

Ciara glared at the mess on the table. "I didn't do that."

Mrs. Bohacek smiled up at her in that I-know-something-you-don't-know way. "Of course you did."

Ciara grumbled and crossed her arms. This woman didn't want her to hide her emotions. Fine. That anger inside simmered up again and the ice block on the table melted and then evaporated, leaving a reddish-brown stain on the tablecloth.

More smiles from the witch. "Ready to learn to use those emotions you're quelling to your advantage?"

"No." She felt like sticking out her tongue and having a tantrum, something she'd never done in her entire life, not even as a child. The tablecloth sparked and lit on fire.

Mrs. Bohacek sat back and smiled, letting the fire spread.

There wasn't a fire extinguisher in sight, only piles of shiny expensive things. "Ack. Quick, throw the tea on it to put it out."

If this is what her emotions did, then poo on them. Ciara lunged for the tea pot, but a gust of wind blew across the table and lifted the pot into the air and out of her reach. It also fanned the flames. It hovered above the table and landed gently in Mrs. Bohacek's lap.

Fine, she'd smother the fire in scones. Again, the breeze took her plan and whisked it away into the waiting arms of the other woman.

She glared at the woman. "Stop that."

A spark jumped from the table and onto the rack of paintings sitting right next to them. An oil cloth covering the nearest work of art ignited.

Mrs. Bohacek raised both eyebrows, but then shrugged. "Uh-oh, I think that DaVinci is one of Jakob's favorites. Too bad."

Now Ciara was starting to lose her cool. She never, ever lost it. "Knock it off."

"Okay." Mrs. Bohacek waved her hand and the painting fell off the rack and into a pile of bundled stacks of hundred Euro notes.

Who the hell kept literal piles of money just laying around?

The closest stack sizzled and smoked, then caught fire like a log. Shit. If they kept this up, Jakob's entire treasure hoard would go up in flames and she'd either die in the fire or he would kill her when he found out she'd done nothing to stop it.

Ciara clenched her fists and took several deep breaths. That only fanned the flames as a breeze blew from her mouth.

"What do you want from me?" she shouted. More paintings lit along with her words.

Mrs. Bohacek stood up and patted Ciara on the back. "You poor thing. Your emotions are all messed up. Usually anger begets fire or ice depending on the emotion behind it in a new magic user. Your mind can't decide what it wants to do."

"I know I'm broken, okay. Tell me how to put out the fire."

"Kiddo, you aren't broken. Maybe a little chipped, but nothing that can't be filled in with some good loving. I ought to know. Now do as I say and close your eyes."

Ciara frowned at her.

"Go on. If you want to save the rest of those paintings, you'll do it." She tipped her head toward the tower of fire.

"Fine." Ciara closed her eyes and saw swirls of red and blue behind her eyelids. She didn't like it one bit.

"Imagine a beautiful vegetable garden." Mrs. Bohacek drew out the syllables, all sing-song-y and fairy godmother-like.

Ciara had never had a garden. Unless you counted Farmville. Then she remembered the area around the haystack Jakob had dropped her into. There had been fresh dirt and lots of growing things there.

"Good, now remember a time when you felt loved and focus your emotions, concentrate on pushing them under the dirt and bubbling it up from the ground."

Love and dirt didn't go together. Dirt wasn't helpful. It got under one's nails and got one's hands smacked at the dinner table for not washing her hands.

Something crackled and crashed next to them. "Hmm, no that's not working. Try again. Search your memories again, find that underlying emotion inside of you."

Ciara peeked out of one eye and saw the flames jumping several feet into the air. Eek. She slammed that eye back shut. What had she been thinking a minute ago?

Oh, right. When Jakob had dropped her in the haystack. And when he'd pulled her out.

The way she'd accidentally straddled him. God, he was so fricking sexy, all hot and hard between her legs.

"That's it. Focus that emotion right there and it will do the work for you. Whatever you're thinking of right now, amp that up."

It's not like she had to try hard to do that. Her mind went straight from that scene to the sizzling kiss. A tingle crackled across her skin from the inside out. Why had she stopped him from doing more?

"Look, you've built up a pile of dirt. Now, ask that earth to help you."

Ciara turned her face away and slowly pried one eye open just in case the flames were doing the dance she'd set them on. Instead she saw dark, loamy earth gurgling up all around her feet.

Mrs. Bohacek nodded. "You've got a natural ability with the earth, but your censorship of your passions has been hiding that. We all favor one element in the beginning. I thought maybe you'd be stronger with fire or ice, since you manifested those elements first, but not so much."

She indicated the pile of dirt that continued to grow and overtake the flames, dousing them as they covered each painting.

"You're saying I did that? That the dirt is under my control?"

Ciara shook her head while the witch in white nodded.

The dirt continued to pile up until the whole rack of paintings were buried. "Make it stop."

"It's doing your bidding, not mine. You make it stop."

Ciara rubbed at her face. This couldn't be real.

"Sooner, rather than later would be good, unless you're ready to ride that earth out of here."

The dirt towered to the ceiling of the cavern, enveloping all the treasure around them. Shit.

She sighed and closed her eyes. She thought of the way Jakob's lips had brushed across hers when he first kissed her. The tingle under her skin resurged and she focused her feelings, asking the dirt to go back into the earth with her mind.

When she peeked to see if anything was happening, the dirt whooshed past her and into the ground at her feet.

"Fantastic. You're well on your way to making nice with the elements. Tea?" The teapot, cups, and snack tray floated back to the table.

She was kind of thirsty. "Are you using wind to move those?"

They sat, and Mrs. Bohacek poured new cups for them both. "Very astute."

"What emotion controls the wind?" Had she really just asked that? She had. She could hardly believe it, but she was buying into this emotion and magic mumbo Dumbo. If elephants can fly, why couldn't she?

Because she wasn't an elephant. She was a chubby wedding planner with no life, no boyfriend, and obviously losing her mental stability.

She wasn't kidding anyone. Her weeks were spent planning happily ever afters for other people. Wes was probably only being nice to her because she made them both money, and the tight rein she'd learned to have on her emotions at a very young age was the one thing she'd been able to control in her life.

Not so much anymore.

The complete disappointment in herself and her life clawed at her insides and threatened to overwhelm her. She'd gotten great at pretending that nothing mattered, nothing got to her when she made her feelings her bitch.

Now that they were bubbling up, like that pile of dirt, she couldn't pick and choose which ones she felt. The lust and excitement she'd felt with Jakob came out just as strong as the underlying fear that no one would ever love her, and the weird mix of guilt and anger her mother evoked.

Ciara covered all those thoughts up with a pile of dirt inside of her head. Then planted pretty flowers on top.

Mrs. Bohacek poured the tea but looked sideways at Ciara while doing it. "It's different for every witch." Her words were soft, like she was testing to see Ciara's reaction to them. "I find the wind element with joy and excitement."

"Ha." See? See! She'd never disdainfully laughed at anyone in her life. But seriously? Joy? "Ha. I don't even know what that word means."

Whoa. Had she said that out loud? It just popped out from nowhere. As did the wind.

It whipped through the cavern, knocking over the paintings she'd just saved, dammit, and making dust devils filled with gold coins.

Dirt and rocks sprinkled down from the ceiling which startled Mrs. Bohacek. She glanced around the caverns and Ciara got the distinct feeling the woman was feeling more than she was seeing.

She folded her arms and spoke, her words cutting through the wind. "Anger works too, but you won't be able to work with the element quite as long when you use a dark emotion. It's extremely taxing."

As if on cue, exhaustion hit Ciara like a Mack truck filled with bricks, sliding down an icy Alaskan glacier. She stumbled back and plopped down into a soft pile of earth that formed around her butt. It snuggled her like a warm blanket. Her vision tunneled and it was really hard to keep her eyes open, or even sit upright.

"I...I didn't ask the dirt to help me. Was that you?"

The witch knelt beside Ciara and stroked her hair. Something had changed about her. She suddenly didn't look as old, her hair was darker, and she glowed with a white aura all around her.

"No, kiddo. That was Jakob's magic. The connection between the two of you is already strong and he's come into his powers now that he has you."

Ciara's words felt heavy in her mouth, like lead marbles. "He doesn't have me. He kidnapped me."

"Yes, I know. It was the best way to get you two together."

What? "You—" Ciara couldn't get any more words out. Darkness was taking her down.

"You're tired now and you will be for a few minutes while we make our getaway. I had hoped to have more time with you."

We? Was Mrs. Bohacek going to help her get out of here or kidnap her too? Ciara had never felt weak like this. It had to more than getting angry and whipping the wind around.

"Let the earth rejuvenate you. It won't take long to absorb my spell, if you let it. Then use what I've taught you to get out of here. Jakob is going to need you. Until he claims you, and gives over his soul, he's very vulnerable."

"Where...are...you..." She had to force the words out.

"Just remember to harness the good feelings and the elements will do whatever you ask."

"...going?"

Ciara couldn't keep her eyes open another millisecond.

The voices around her faded to muffled whispers. Wait. Voices?

"Come, my love. Jakob is battling those fucking Galla dragons right now. I damn sure hope this plan of yours works." A deep rumbling voice filtered through the darkness surrounding her. "If they get his soul shard—"

"They won't. Jakob is strong, and has become even stronger now."

At least she recognized Mrs. Bohacek's voice. Or rather the voice of the beautiful goddess-like woman Mrs. Bohacek had transformed into.

"Yeah. Good thing I decided to let him come into his power on sight of this pretty mate you found for him. He should have claimed her right then and there."

But who was this other person? A man, but who, and where had he come from?

"How was he supposed to know that?"

Ooh. Mrs. B was getting snippy with Mr. Man.

"Instinct. I knew with you."

His words weren't sharp and argumentative as Ciara expected, but soft and placating.

It worked.

"Yes, lover, you did. And I fought you every inch after that."

He chuckled. "Those were the good old days."

Ciara felt like she was a voyeur to a very intimate moment. Not like she could do anything about it.

"Come now. Jakob is on the right path now. Off to your other sons. I have just the woman in mind for —"

The energy in the room popped and the voices were gone. The blackness around Ciara receded and she pried her eyes open. She didn't sit up for a few minutes. The warm earth around her did feel nice. She stayed put. The pretty green dress she'd been given was probably ruined though.

She sat up and stretched. Mrs. Bohacek was gone. So was whomever was with her. Her lover. Ciara had a feeling he was a very powerful being. Maybe even a dragon like Jakob.

Well, screw both of them for leaving her.

Now to get the hell out of here.

If any of this day was real, and for the moment she was going with the presumption that it was, then she had some badass powers that could help her escape any cage. Even a golden lined one like Jakob's lair.

Ciara stood and dusted herself off. She looked around the caverns until she found exactly what she was looking for. A crack in the rock wall.

It was too high up for her to reach, even on her tippy toes. There were several old wooden chests nearby and if she stood on them, she could be face to face with her escape route.

The chest looked really heavy. No time like the present to see if the new magical skills she'd acquired were real or all a weird dream. She closed her eyes and envisioned the garden near the haystack again. "Okay, dirt. Let's play nice. Lift me up."

The ground underneath her went soft and she had to crouch to keep her balance, but it piled up beneath her feet, lifting her into the air.

"Damn skippy." She came eye to eye with the crack in the wall. Yes, behind that hole in the rock was dirt, exactly like what she stood on. Perfect.

Ciara pressed her fingers into the crack and felt ridiculous, but she asked the what she wanted it to do. "Hi, dirt. Could you please spread out a bit and create a space for me to crawl through? I need to get to the surface."

Nothing.

Oh, right. She had to use her happy thoughts too. She was pretty mad at Jakob for leaving her down here, and Mrs. Bohacek could ride her witchy broom to hell. There was only one other person in her life who gave her the warm fuzzies.

She closed her eyes, took a deep breath, and thought of

Wes. His perfect smile, his perfect clothes, that wink that gave her nervous flutters.

Little bits of dirt and rock moved under her fingers and the crack spread, but nowhere near enough for her and her big butt and boobs to fit into.

"God dammit all to hell. Fuck a god damn duck."

A zip of tingles raced across her skin, a physical manifestation of her frustration. She smacked the wall and growled. "Why don't you just open? Would I have to do, say open Sesame?"

The earth split in front of her and she was propelled forward into the crevice, sure she was about to crash to her death. A tunnel opened up in front of her and the tower of dirt beneath her feet pushed her into the ground like she was a gopher on crack. Chunks of dirt and who knows what else fell into her hair and eyes.

She flailed her arms out, dragging her hands, trying to slow her progress, but got only scrapes and scratches for her effort.

Mrs. Bohacek did say her negative emotions were very powerful, but this was ridiculous. She didn't even know where she was going, or which direction was up.

She went careening forward trying her best to focus on an upward momentum. She could feel her energy flagging again. "Please let me make it to the surface. I don't want to die down here buried where no one will find me."

That little bit of fear took hold. She slammed sideways into the rocks.

The dirt beneath her feet continue to bubble up but the rock in front of her no longer opened up a way for her to get out.

She very purposefully slowed her breathing and pushed the panic back down. Everything stilled around her.

The little rabbit hole she'd created around herself gave her only a few inches to move in any direction. She scratched at the wall in front of her and watched the dirt trickle sideways past her face. That meant up was to her right. Thanks, gravity.

She twisted until she was on her hands and knees. There was no way of knowing how far away from the surface she was, but she had to figure out a way to keep going.

Somewhere, possibly only a few feet above her, she heard movement. Scratching on the ground, a thud and a tussle.

No, it was more than that. Someone was fighting. She strained to hear more. Yes, she couldn't make out the voices, but there were definitely growls and screeches happening not far away.

That had to be where Jakob had hurried off to. She kind of thought, maybe even hoped a little, that the alarm and his leaving her was a ruse. A way to get her to reveal the relic Jakob had such a hard on for.

A crash and—God, was that a fire bomb she just heard?— sounded above her and rattled her dirt cocoon. Who or what was Jakob fighting up there, a Panzer division?

CIARA GULPED, trying to push a whole new fear down. The necklace she wore lit up, illuminating the space around her. She covered it with her hand, not wanting to see any creepy crawlies that might fall into her hair. The ground shook again and a roar that was only barely muffled by the thickness of the soil went straight to Ciara's bones.

She needed to get out of here, now.

She dug her fingers into the dirt in front of her and clawed until chunks began falling away. She imagined the great green dragon fighting against knights in not so shining armor. "Please, move a little more."

The ground didn't open up like it had before, but each handful she grabbed and pushed away came out easier. The tiny amount of space she had around her quickly filled with clumps of dirt. Thank goodness for the light from the necklace or she'd be feeling awfully claustrophobic. Wait, up ahead, yes, a pinprick of moonlight shined through the ground. She wiggled her butt and legs, inching herself up. Her arm must look like one of Michael Jackson's Thriller zombies coming out of the ground. One more boost and her head and shoulders surfaced too.

The grass around her was stained with black, burnt smudges. Ew. She didn't want to touch or smell whatever it was that used to be.

She glanced around, looking for both the danger and Jakob. She heard his deep growl before she saw him. There, directly behind her, a hundred yards into the field next to the villa. The same green dragon who had swept her away was rearing up and slashing at very scary looking black lizard-like creatures.

Only they weren't anyone's pet lizards. They were only half Jakob's size, but there were so many.

The dragon whipped its tail around, and huge spikes at the end caught one of the lizard people in the face. The ugly lizard thing disintegrated, leaving only that same ashy stain on the ground where it had been.

Holy crap balls, Batman. There were at least two dozen of those black marks all over the ground between her and Jakob. He'd killed so many, and yet there were still at least ten more attacking him.

Jesus, Mary and Joseph, and all the saints. She was getting the hell out of here.

Ciara climbed the rest of the way out of the ground, and the hole instantly filled in behind her. The only trace was the lack of grass. She turned and fled as fast as her bare feet would carry her away from the melee. She had no idea where she was going, but there had to be another house, or a town, or something nearby. Right? Right.

She was no runner, and she got a stitch in her side before she even broke a sweat. She didn't want to slow down, but what if one of those things came after her?

A dirt road wound around the edge of the area in front of the Villa. Maybe if she stuck to it, a car or a wagon, given by the antiquated look of the road, would come by.

Ciara ignored the pricks and pains her feet were enduring on the walk – jog – walk she was pushing herself to do. As soon as she got home, she was getting a pedicure. And a security system, and some mace, and maybe a Taser. Oh, and therapy.

Although, if she told anyone the truth about what had happened to her in the past twenty-four hours, they would lock her up in a loony bin. Because that's what her story would be, Looney Tunes.

DEMON DRAGONS

*J*akob used the momentum of tunneling up from the cavern to propel him into the sky. The instant he had the room, he unfurled his wings and circled the villa. He caught a colorful flash out of the corner of his eye. It wasn't a demon dragon, but when he turned to see what it was, he found the black enemy.

The inky black bastards were digging up his garden like Peter Rabbits from hell. Of course, it was strategically placed directly above his lair. They were rapidly creating a deep crater in the earth. If there had only been a handful of them, he wouldn't be worried that they would reach the cavern, but there had to be at least fifty, digging, clawing, and desperate to get to his treasure.

He'd destroyed ten times that many in battle, but not all at the same time. This was the largest horde of evil he'd ever seen gathered in one place. Fuck. He'd sent Steele away earlier that day and now he had no backup.

The majority of the wyrms dug, but ten or so standing around the edge lifted their faces to the sky, searching him out, hissing. They couldn't fly with their minuscule wings, but Jakob also couldn't destroy them from up here. Destroy them he would.

Nothing would touch his treasure.

Nothing had ever touched what was his.

Except a sexy, sneaky, sumptuous witch.

Not the time or the place to think about her and the way she made him want to – grrr. Get your head in the game, dumb dragon, or you'll never get the chance to play all those dirty games with her and that plump ass.

Jakob roared, gathering his focus again. Never in his memory had a horde attacked a Wyvern's home directly. It was as if they knew his villa was vulnerable at the moment. Normally, he would have had a squad of dragon warriors in and around the seat of the green dragon stronghold.

Even so, they'd made a huge mistake coming here. He'd have a good time showing them why, and work off some of the frustration that had worked its way into his muscles in the past two days.

He dove, tucking in tight, and screeched towards the clump gathered at the edge of the crater. He slashed the throat of the first demon dragon and caught two more with the spikes on his tail. Power and strength buzzed through his bloodstream, rippled across his scales.

Oh, yeah. This was going to be fun.

The soul shard at his throat hummed with energy. A force he hadn't known before flowed through him. The outline of each wyrm sharpened. He could hear their ragged breathing even beneath the shrieks of anger. Their acrid scent burned his nostrils, the flavor of their blackened blood stains surged across his tongue.

The power of his dragon swelled inside and stretched,

spreading from nose to tail, from wing tip to wing tip. His wings pounded the air as he swooped up over the horde again. This dragon form was at least twice or even three times the size of any of them, and felt enormous, like the first time he'd ever shifted as a youngling.

Wherever he was receiving this new power from, he'd take it, and use it to defeat anything standing in his way. As long as the surge of intensity would last, Jakob would take advantage of it.

He twisted in the air and landed hard, like Thor's hammer to the ground. He swiped and clawed and crushed any within his reach. More popped up in their places. The spittle of fire, their lowly attempts to harm him were futile. The ground became dark, littered with the black stains left behind by the wyrm's death.

Two of the demon dragons used their powerful legs to leap onto his back, blasting his armored scales with their fire. He bellowed and shook one off, but the other sunk its claws into the flesh beneath his scales. Jakob rolled crushing the thing out of existence.

Another jumped on his side and shredded the thin skin of his right wing. Bastard, be damned. That pissed him the hell off.

He kicked the demon dragon hard enough to send it careening into the crater. Several of its cohorts scattered, but only for a moment. The battle did not seem to be deterring them from digging toward his treasure.

Jakob called upon the element of earth that his kind commanded, and a wall of soil burst up and toppled over, burying the demon dragons who were centermost in the crater. It didn't kill them, as the earth element was for life not death. But it did hamper their efforts long enough for him to finish three more of them off.

His teeth, tail, and claws alone were not enough to defeat so many. He hated to do it, but called upon the plants to assist him.

Several of the bastards closest to him were instantly strangled by tomato vines, hampering their ability to use their fire. They scratched and tore at the fragile plants, giving him enough time to run them through with his talons.

For every slimy piece of shit he turned to dust, three more appeared out of the darkness.

What the hell were they doing here?

Didn't they have a village to plague?

That, he knew how to deal with. Save the humans from the monsters from hell, without them knowing. That was what he had trained for his entire life. Those were the countless number of battles he had fought and won. But this—an attack directly on him and his land—was entirely a different situation.

They knew it too. Their sole focus was in burrowing through the ground, and they didn't seem to care how many had to die for them to continue the mission.

No demon dragon had ever been interested in treasure. They had only ever been hell-bent on destruction.

What the hell was down there that they wanted so badly?

Fucking hell.

Ciara.

She was the only new variable.

She was a much more powerful witch, and a darker one than he suspected, if she had demon dragons under her control.

He couldn't believe under all that sweet sexiness lay a black witch.

Nope. No way.

Her little fits of elemental magic had been pure.

If these little fuckers weren't working for her, they had to be after her. He'd be damned if anyone besides him would kidnap her.

God dammit. They were after her for the same reason he had been. She had the First Dragon's relic.

The dumbass that he was, he'd been so star struck with her allure, like she was a fucking succubus, that he hadn't even gotten the relic back.

Now it was an even more jeopardy than when she'd stolen it for herself. He was going to kill her. But first, he had to kill another couple dozen demon dragons.

He let that anger fuel his magic, only needing the short burst it would give him to slay the remaining beasts. He roared, and the earth opened beneath the horde. They tumbled and fell in droves, surprised, giving him the advantage.

Jakob jumped into the hole and pummeled the demon dragons with his body and rocks from the earth. He was down to only a few remaining, when something grabbed at his magic. His stomach jolted, sure for a split second he was falling uncontrollably.

The licorice scent of Ciara smacked him upside the head. Jakob glanced around ready to snatch her and take flight. No Ciara popped into view.

He opened his senses wide, searching for her, sending spirals of magic through the earth to find her. The connection was nearly instantaneous.

Ciara remained underground in his lair, although not

alone and definitely in trouble. God damn it. There was no fucking way anyone had gotten into the lair. Except someone had. For the second time in as many days.

Ciara, tell me who is with you. Are you in danger?

No response. Not only was there no answer from her, his words were blocked, as if a wall of soundproofed insulation wrapped around her mind.

He could feel her energy and magic through the earth but couldn't reach her. He sent the earth to surround her in its healing warmth until he could get to her.

His distracted state allowed the remaining enemy to escape, and they were headed straight for the closest human town. If he went after Ciara, he subjected the town to death and destruction. His soul revolted at the idea of leaving her exposed to danger.

First Dragon help him.

That same zip of fire and ice he'd experienced when he held Ciara in his arms raced across his body again. The soul shard at his throat beamed a bright green light into the night. The beam focused and pointed back toward the part of the garden where he'd first dropped Ciara and rolled in the hay with her. A hand reached up out of the dirt like a zombie in an 80's pop star music video. The hand was followed by shoulders and a blonde head.

Holy shit. Ciara was crawling out of the ground. To come out in that spot, she had to have tunneled through the earth above the lair the same as he had. There was only one way to do that. She had to use the gift of the green dragon warriors. Earth elemental magic.

No fucking way.

Fire, wind, and now power over the earth element. No witch in thousands of years, not since the First Dragon's mate, the White Witch, had control of more than one element. And yet here, Ciara controlled three out of the four. It had to be because she had stolen the relic. There was no other explanation.

At least she looked unharmed and alone. The necklace at her throat glowed in answer to his own shard. She bolted toward the front of the villa and the one road that led toward the town.

Stupid, crazy, fascinating woman

She wouldn't escape him.

The demon dragon closest to Jakob lunged at him, reaching for his soul shard. It got a hold of the cord and yanked.

This was the weirdest fucking battle he'd ever been in, on the weirdest god damned day of his life. What the hell did a demon dragon want with a soul shard? Well, Jakob certainly wasn't going to give up his. He ripped the head off of the demon dragon with his teeth and spit it to the side. By the time he'd done that, Ciara was out of sight.

The demon dragons around him took off across the field like a pack of hounds on the hunt. Jakob took to the air and followed them into the field adjoining the villa. He slashed and sliced, working his way through the final dirty dozen. He was down to the remaining three when two of them pushed their comrade forward into him, using the block to escape.

He'd catch them both soon enough, well before they got anywhere near the town or Ciara.

Jakob snared the sacrificial demon dragon in his claw and stared into its beady little eyes. He growled his frustration at it. *Where are your friends going?*

Not like he expected the thing to answer, it was no smarter than a trained monkey.

"Let go."

Huh. That was new. Add talking demon dragon to the list of bizarro shit he'd eventually have to report to the AllWyr council. If it could say that much, maybe he should imprison it and interrogate it later. Think of the intel they could get knowing the enemy could talk. *Tell me where your friends are going.*

"Get witch." The demon scratched at Jakob's claw trying to get away, desperation in its eyes.

What witch?

"Your witch."

Rage burned through Jakob's soul, burning him from the inside out. He squeezed the demon dragon's throat until its head popped off like a dandelion. It disintegrated into black ash that didn't even hit the ground before Jakob took three running steps bolting into the air to search for Ciara. No demon dragon would ever touch her. She was his.

Forever.

Fuck.

What?

One woman for him, forever. That was not a thing. Not one he was willing to think about right now, anyway.

Jakob opened his senses wide again, asking the foliage and flora of the countryside to help him locate Ciara. The stones and trees pulled him toward the small town a few minutes away. Exactly where he thought she had been headed. He couldn't have planned that any better.

The town was centuries old, even older than he was. Most of the residents came from trusted families, in fact his entire household staff lived there. No human in the town was old enough to remember the last demon dragon attack. Jakob himself had been so young then that he hadn't even been able to shift yet. His father had let him observe the battle though. He learned his first lesson in military strategy that day. Always have a reliable wing man.

Not a single hair on a human head had been harmed that day, because of the coordinated attack by the Green Wyvern and his second. But Jakob's father might have been badly injured, or even killed, if his second in command hadn't been at his back. Jakob watched the killing blow by a demon dragon that day get deflected by another powerful dragon.

The Green Dragon warriors, now under Jakob's command, were just as powerful as days gone by. He was the complete idiot who had sent them all away.

It would've been a hell of a lot smarter to have an entire battalion on the search for the First Dragon's relic. His ego would have been knocked down a few notches, but his IQ could have gone up, if he had asked the other Wyverns for their help too.

But no.

He didn't want to look like a dumbass for losing the relic in the first place.

Instead, he was the worst Wyvern in a millennium.

His father always had so much faith, such high expectations for him. Too bad he wasn't living up to a single one of them.

The town came into view, and Jakob spotted one of the demon dragons slipping between two buildings at the edge of the settlement. He didn't yet see the other one, or Ciara, but he knew they were near. He could feel them.

If the beacon from his soul shard was any indication, they were near the town square in the center. He was set to follow the light, which still astounded him, but it left the other demon dragon to wreak havoc wherever it wanted to. Which, of course, is exactly what it did.

Its black shadow crept up the side of the home and pulled an unlatched window open.

Normally, the townsfolk didn't need to worry about locking their doors or their windows. The worst crime in this rural area was someone not paying their bar tab on time. That's what happened when they were protected by dragons.

The scent of a brand-new human life hit Jakob before he saw the baby. The thought of what the demon dragon could do to that little soul punched Jakob square in the esophagus. He couldn't swallow past the thought of that evil piece of shit spreading its plague to the child.

Fear gripped that lump in Jakob's throat and held on tight until he had the demon dragon in his talons. He shredded the bastard before it could even take its next breath and spew fire at him. His ashes scattered on the wind created by the powerhouse of his wings pushing them through the air.

He landed softly, because the residents had not yet noticed any disturbance in town and awoken.

Something near his heart went all squishy, as he stared in at the babe. Its life force was strong, but Jakob blew some of his healing dragon's breath over the child, just in case. The gentle puff of green smoke made it sneeze but did not wake up.

He would have to sire one of these of his own one day. Every Wyvern needed a first son to continue the lineage of leadership. He'd rather have a daughter. One with sparkling green eyes and lovely blonde curls, just like Ciara's.

Too bad dragons didn't have daughters.

If he didn't get his head out of his butt and go save her

from the other demon dragon, this cozy little future life he'd envisioned would be nothing more than a silly dream.

A scream wrenched through the night and Jakob saw the body of a demon dragon tossed into the air like it was bouncing on a trampoline, spinning and flipping, but not having a good time.

What was his witch doing now?

Jakob bounded over the nearest rooftops and into the town square. Ciara was huddled under the metal awning of a payphone. She had her eyes scrunched tight and the phone outstretched as if it were a weapon.

The demon dragon crashed onto the cobblestone in front of her. It lifted its head, shook it like a dog, and growled at her. "I kill you."

"Eek." Ciara waved the phone again, and the demon dragon was blown across the square, tumbling cartwheel style, reminding Jakob of a children's cartoon.

It would be funny, if it wasn't so, so... fucking hot.

She was using the wind to keep her enemy at bay. The dumbass demon kept getting back up and rushing at her again and again. Each time it took a little flight up in the air, ass over tail, and once even spinning like a disco queen, encased in a dust devil she created.

Jakob leaned against the nearest building. He could watch this all day.

But after a few more blows, Ciara wilted against the phone box. He could practically see her energy throwing up the white flag and waving it.

The demon dragon knew it too. On this next run at her, it dodged her attempts to push it away and blew a stream of fire at her. Jakob moved to throw up a wall of dirt to block the fire, but she beat him to it. That act of magic took her remaining strength and she slumped to the ground, falling hard on her ass, but still clinging to the phone handset.

Jakob opened a hole in the ground beneath the demon dragon. It was sucked into the earth and before it could scramble out Jakob was there spearing it through the skull with the spikes on his tail. It disintegrated to black ash that Jakob buried in the ground.

"Go away, leave me alone." A light breeze smacked Jakob in the face.

Ciara. I'm here now. Don't—

Jakob lifted into the air and dropped on his back six feet away.

Ciara was again on her feet, trembling and wobbling but with the wind whipping her hair, and fire in her eyes. "I said, leave me alone."

What a woman.

ESCAPEGOAT

*C*iara jog-walked away from the villa and the battle dragon-Jakob was immersed in with the black snake people. She could not put enough distance between all of that nightmare and herself.

It was a good half an hour before she found anything resembling civilization. But finally, she saw lights up ahead. She pushed herself even more and made it into the town, if it could even be called that, in another ten or fifteen minutes.

This place was the definition of a sleepy little village, and it would be quaint if she didn't need to find a live human being with a phone. Not a single light was on in any of the windows. The place was dark, save for the streetlamps.

In a minute, she was going to just start shouting to see if anyone was alive in this place. She walked a few more feet, beginning to hobble a bit, should anyone want to look at her feet. Then, lo and behold, a payphone, so old Superman probably had changed outfits in it. She limped across the street, sure she was leaving bloody footprints as she went. The phone booth didn't have a door, more like metal hood to protect it from the elements. She grabbed the handset and thanked the Lord there was a dial tone. But how did one place a collect call from a foreign country?

She punched the zero hoping to get an English-speaking operator. A man's voice came across the line and said a whole streak of words she didn't understand.

"Hello? Do you speak English by any chance?"

"Yes, a little. How can I help?"

"I need to make a call to the US."

"Do you have a calling card?"

How was she supposed to explain that she been kidnapped by a dragon and left her wallet at home? "No, is there any other way to pay for the call?"

"I can connect you to a service that can provide you with minutes over the phone if you have a credit card."

Once again, no wallet or purse. What she did have was a mind like a plastic trap. She used her Willingham Weddings business credit card so often on flower vendors, cake makers, and last-minute seamstresses, that she had the number memorized. Of course, her mother would flip out when she saw a bill for an international calling card. But dammit, this was an emergency.

She could practically hear her mother's voice saying, "your lack of planning does not constitute an emergency on my part."

Not like she could have planned ahead for kidnapping. "Yes, I will do that option. Thank you."

"Connecting you now."

After a series of beeps and an automated voice, thankfully in English, Ciara entered the digits on the phone. She was given one hundred minutes for the price of one hundred crowns. She'd have to figure out how much that was later. She punched in the 01 to get through to America and then her mother's phone number. The line rang and rang.

Crud, what time was it in America? She didn't even know what time it was here. She wasn't even a hundred percent sure where here was. She was most likely in the Czech Republic, because Jakob had said his villa was not far from Prague. But how far was not far for someone who could fly thousands of miles?

Ciara figured that Europe was probably about six hours ahead of the East Coast, and it looked to be pretty late at night since nothing in this village was open.

She was sure she was going to get her mother's voicemail in another ring or two and thought about who else she could call.

"Why are you calling me at this hour Ciara Tara Mosley – Willingham?" Her mother's voice came through as clear as if they were standing ten feet apart. While the average person wouldn't hear the ire in her mother's voice, because her mother didn't allow that, Ciara cringed.

How had her mother known it was her? "Mother, I'm sorry, but this is an emergency."

"You know how I feel about your emergencies."

Yes, she did. "No, mother. This is actually an emergency I've been —"

"Call me in the morning at a reasonable hour, and when you have resolved your little crisis. I have clients who will need your attention."

Before Ciara could even say the word kid, much less kidnapped, the line had gone dead.

She looked at the phone, and frost crystals grew over the handset.

Should have known better.

Well, shit.

Who else could she call? Who else's number did she actually know? Without her cell phone, she was missing part of her brain.

But she wasn't kidding anybody by pretending she didn't know at least one name and phone number by heart.

Yeah, she would call him. He was probably worried sick about her.

She dialed up the operator again and went through the same routine and found that her short call to her mother had used up a third of her minutes. She would need this call to Wes to be succinct. She rehearsed in her head what she would say before she dialed the number, and then waited for the ring. The phone rang, and rang again, and rang another three times. No, she couldn't get his voicemail. She hung up the phone, picked it right back up, and went through the whole routine again. The phone rang, and it rang, and it rang again.

"Hello?"

Ciara could barely hear him. The thump thump thumping of loud music, and so many voices, drowned his out. "Wes? Wes, can you hear me?"

"Ciara? Is that you, babe?"

"Yes." She stuck one finger in her ear and pressed the handset tight against her face, trying to hear him even though the noise was on his end. "I am in Prague."

"You're a frog?"

She'd rehearsed this, but it didn't do any good to tell him she was in Prague kidnapped and needed him to come get her, if he couldn't understand what she was saying. "No, I am... in... Prague."

"If you're sick, doll, your mother will kill you."

Dammit. "I'm not sick. I'm in the Czech Republic."

"Yes, I'll check with her."

Dammit dammit dammit.

"I've been kidnapped." She shouted the words but doubted it would help at this point.

"A nap is probably a good idea."

Ciara banged her hand against the metal awning. Then another voice came across the line. "Hey, can I buy you a drink?"

What kind of a place was Wes at?

"Hey doll, gotta run. See you on Thursday. I think you'll like this place."

The phone went dead and Ciara stared at handset.

That had not gone like she expected it to, not even a little bit. She'd imagined Wes rushing to the airport and booking a ticket to Prague to come and get her, and they'd live happily ever after.

Boy, had she been wrong.

What the hell was she going to do now?

She supposed she could just hang out here in the area near the phone. It appeared to be some sort of a town square. Maybe in the morning people gathered here to, what, sell their wares?

In a few more hours it would be morning in America, she could try to call again then.

Ciara's stomach rumbled, and she wished she would have eaten some of those tea cakes Mrs. Bohacek had. She was pretty hungry. Her stomach growled again, this time a whole hell of a lot louder.

Ciara swallowed and put one hand on her belly. That sound had not been her insides wishing for French fries.

She turned slowly, feeling like the TDTL girl in the horror movies. Too Dumb To Live.

Oh, yeah. There was something out of a nightmare behind her, she could feel its hot breath on the back of her neck. Breath that smelled like poo mixed with pig guts.

"I get witch." Its voice was slimier than a drunk used car salesman on the last day of the year.

Was he talking about her?

See? TDTL. Of course he was talking about her.

The real question was, what the hell was she going to do about it?

Fear curdled her brain like rotten chocolate milk, but somewhere in the gooey center was Mrs. Bohacek's voice. "Use what you've learned."

What she'd learned was this world was not what she'd thought it was. Oh, and she was a witch.

A smart witch.

Ciara stuck her hand out and pointed toward the sky. "Look, a big purple dragon."

She hoped against hope that had distracted the monster for just the second she needed. She pivoted and pointed at it, the handset for the phone still in her fist. *Wind help me now. Pretty please.*

The black snakelike creature flew into the air and landed on top of the metal awning with a crash. Ciara screamed, partly out of surprise and partly because it had worked. That was short lived.

The thing reached for her and snagged one shoulder of the dress, which tore when she blew it into the sky again.

The first wave of exhaustion hit her, but nothing like it had in Jakob's lair. She stood firm in her spot, not letting it seep into her bones.

The beast came at her again and again, each time she blew it away like Wile E. Coyote standing in front of a wind machine. The waves of fatigue grew bigger with each of her efforts. She maybe had one more push in her but knew that a tsunami of tiredness would hit her.

Either she could use the wind again and run away or try something different. Mrs. Bohacek had said she had an affinity for the earth element. She had gotten out of that stupid cavern. Earth it was.

She crouched to the ground but miscalculated and hit it hard with her butt.

The demon thing must have taken her new position as weakness, because it charged at her again, but this time fire spewed from its mouth, exactly like what she thought a dragon could do.

Shit, shite, shat.

In her mind, she envisioned a wall of dirt, and in reality, one flew up between her and the fire. She had every intention of burying the bastard in the ground but she couldn't seem to move. That tsunami had hit her.

She was going to die. Her gravestone would read – Eaten, and not in the fun way. Didn't that just sum up her whole damn life.

Another monster swooped down and Ciara shut her eyes tight waiting for the first chomp. Maybe if it bit off her head she wouldn't feel the pain.

No pain came. Was she already dead?

She took a breath, but dead people didn't breathe as far she knew.

A voice rumbled around inside of her head. Adrenaline pumped through her blacking out anything but her fight or flight instinct.

"Go away, and leave me alone." Even the effort of saying those words sent her into a gray tunnel of oblivion.

No, she would not die this way.

She stood again, not knowing where the energy came from, but using it anyway. She was operating a thousand percent on instinct now. The wind whipped around her, helping to hold her up. She shot it out in all directions, hoping to blast her enemies to kingdom come.

That voice was back in her head again, but this time it was laughing. Not like Snidely Whiplash, but like… Jakob.

She rubbed her eyes and saw the big green dragon sauntering toward her. She couldn't have been happier to see him if he was Puff the Magic Dragon.

Ciara. You were magnificent.

He snuffled her with that great snout of his. She smacked it. "Jesus, Mary, and Jiminy Cricket. I thought you were one of those things. And what the hell were those things? Quit talking in my head and turn back into a man right this second."

The adrenaline that had been thumbing through her veins and arteries and brain and fingertips crashed. Tears trickled out of her eyes and she blinked, not wanting to cry in front of him.

He shimmered and shifted back into the sexy ass man she knew.

She had two choices here. Stay mad, fall apart and cry, or jump his bones.

One of these things was going to happen. If she fell apart, she looked like a big fat baby, and he'd simply carry her back to his lair where she would probably die.

But if she jumped his bones, she wasn't sure she would be able to look herself in the eye in the morning.

Well, she'd deal with that in the morning. Guess that decision was made.

She grabbed his shirt and yanked him to her.

He opened his mouth, not to kiss her but to speak. She slapped her hand over his lips and said, "shut up and kiss me."

He raised one eyebrow, pulled her hand down off of his mouth, and did as he was told.

Boy, oh, boy, did he do as he was told.

Jakob grabbed her around the waist and yanked her tight to his body. His tongue dipped in and out of her mouth, mimicking exactly what she wanted other parts of their bodies to do.

Jakob apparently did too, because she could feel his erection pressing against her stomach. Either that or he had a – no, no that was definitely a long hard dick in his pants, and he was happy to see her.

He pushed her up against the metal awning and reached down, lifting her left leg and wrapping it around his hip. He ground against her, pushed his hand into her hair and growled her name.

"Ciara. You fucking taste like licorice and fire."

That adrenaline she thought was gone sang a song of exultation as it rushed back through her body. She didn't even care that they were outside, that anyone who peeked out a window would see them dry humping in the middle of the square. She wanted this man with a ferocity she'd never known.

He grabbed her other leg and lifted, ripping the skirt of the dress so she straddled him. Sweet baby Cheeze Whiz.

If he were anything other than a guy who could turn into a dragon, she'd be worried they were both going crashing to the ground. No man picked her up, she wasn't that lithe, wispy kind of girl. But she didn't need to worry about the insecurities attached to her size with him. God that felt amazing.

Desperation, adrenaline, and lust were all in the driver's seat. She wrapped her legs around his waist, her arms around his neck, and her tongue around his teeth.

All she wanted right now was to crawl inside of him, or rather have him inside of her. The part of her conscience that was flipping out, telling her to take it slow, and called her mean names was outmatched by the happy, excited, let's get laid part.

In fact, the horny cheerleader for team sexy times sat on sane good girl and squashed her into the dirt.

Ciara shoved one hand into Jakob's soft hair and scraped her fingers across the back of his neck and got the growl she hoped for. Jakob sucked her bottom lip into his mouth and bit hard enough to send a pleasure pain shooting through her.

"Ah, my dirty witch likes it a little rough, huh? That I can do, sweetheart."

He moved his mouth from her lips down to her neck, sucking and nipping at her. His hands kneaded her butt and his hips pushed at her rhythmically.

"Mmm, yes." Each scrape of his teeth across her bare skin sent shivers through her body, up and down her spine, sparking her lust for him. "You need more hands, so you can do that thing where you hold my wrists over my head."

A pile of stones rose up underneath Ciara, creating a seat at exactly the right height. Jakob grabbed both her arms and shoved them against the metal at her back. He didn't raise his face, only buried it deeper into the crook of her neck.

"Tell me right fucking now if you don't want this, Ciara."

Uh, duh. She answered with a whimper. Shoot, that's not what she wanted to do. She wanted to shout her yes, yes, yes, so the whole village heard. But each time his tongue licked over her collarbone, each rasp of his teeth, every biting draw of her skin into his mouth sent her body into complete reactionary mode.

Her mouth to brain connection frizzled and nothing more than moans made it out.

He brought his face up to hers. The green of his eyes had gone dark, his eyelids hooded, and he stared straight into her soul. "Say it, Ciara. Say you want this, want me."

"Mmm." Whimper. Nope. Try that again. "Ya....uh...esss."

"Say. It." He was a wild predator, focused only on her and what he wanted from her.

"I..." she more than wanted him and his body. She needed both. Ciara swallowed and pulled in a shaky breath, recovering from the unabashed desire enough to say what they both wanted to hear. "I want you, right here. Right now."

His eyes went incredibly darker, his pupils elongated, and Ciara saw the dragon inside, rising to the surface. Brilliant green scales rippled across his skin and the night lit up with a green light. The crystal at his neck sent ribbons of magic and light into the darkness like the Aurora Borealis.

The necklace she wore matched it, but with sparkles of dazzling white.

Jakob captured both her wrists in one of his hands and ripped open his belt and pants with the other. She tilted her hips forward, trying to meet him, show him with her body that she wanted him.

He pushed aside the torn bits of fabric from her dress and positioned his cock at her entrance but froze. "Where the hell are your panties?"

"Don't stop now, dragon." She wiggled against him, trying to get him to move. She'd changed out of them hours ago when Mrs. Bohacek had given her this dress. "I'm not wearing any."

"That is sexy as fuck." He finally, finally pressed forward, sinking his cock into her, filling her, stretching her around him.

"Oh, God." The guy didn't need an ego boost, but he was so big, and it felt so damn good. She closed her eyes and laid her head back, reveling in the way his body matched hers so perfectly.

Jakob lowered his head, latching his teeth around her collarbone, but not biting down. Then he thrust and withdrew, thrust again giving them both what they wanted, what they needed.

MINE

Ciara's whimpers went on a war path directly from Jakob's ears, down his spine and straight to his cock. Being inside of her wasn't enough. He needed to possess her body and soul. God, how he wanted to take it slow, make sure she was getting as much fucking pleasure from their joining as he was. But he simply couldn't help himself.

Every thrust inside of her sent the same message through his brain. Mine.

Mine.

Mine.

She was beautiful, she was lush, she was a goddess— mother nature come to life in his arms. She was his.

The skin at her neck was the sweetest thing he'd ever tasted. Addictive. She would be covered with bruises and bite marks, all that he promised himself he would soothe, after he claimed her.

He couldn't.

He had to.

No dragon since before his father's generation had

claimed a mate. Not for seven hundred years. Because the only woman a dragon could claim was his true mate.

Dragons no longer had true mates.

Companions. Human women who one could have a relationship with, maybe even children. But not one that he loved, not one whom he was created to love and be loved by in return.

Real love was no more. Not for him nor any of his kind.

The draw to Ciara was undeniable. Every raw instinct screamed the truth.

He'd known it from the second he saw her, he just hadn't wanted to believe it. Now he couldn't deny the rush of need that went well beyond lust. It hit him in the chest, directly behind his soul shard, traveling through him like a landslide.

He needed her more than the earth needed the sun. The deepest, most primal part of him—the place inside where his dragon came from—pushed him to mark her, claim her, make her his mate.

"Jakob, yes, yes." Ciara keened, and her body tightened around his.

Thank God. Because with this rush of emotion, the pure compulsion he had to fuck her, mingle his scent with hers, his essence with her being, he wasn't going to last much longer.

He'd be damned if he let the primitive drive to own her completely make him into an ass. She would come long and hard with his cock buried deep inside of her. She would be his then, and she'd love every minute of it.

Jakob reached one hand between their bodies and slid his fingers into her slick folds. With each thrust into her he stroked his fingers across her plump clit.

She gasped and arched her back, seeking more from him. He longed to whisper all the dirty things he wanted to do to her body, but there was no fucking way his mouth and teeth were moving from her throat.

He bit down harder, not yet enough to break the skin, but so she would know he was never letting her go. His cock begged for release, his mouth watered, and his mind barked for him to finish it, to claim her for his own.

Not. Yet.

"Please, please. Harder. Ahh, harder."

The perfect woman for him. Fucking perfect.

Jakob bit down, pistoned his hips, and pinched her clit until her body bucked beneath him.

Her body gave him the final signal he needed, a flutter of her pussy, on the verge of complete bliss. He sunk his teeth into her tender flesh, the dragon part of him marking her so everyone would know she was his. His soul tethered to hers, his life given for hers, two made one.

Ciara cried out, the bite pushing her over the edge, the orgasm slamming into her, taking him with her. Jakob poured himself into her, letting the ecstasy of being with her finally take over. His hips jerked and his jaw locked onto her.

Ciara's fists opened and closed, still held fast in Jakob's grip. Her pussy clenched around his cock, drawing out both of their orgasms. Stars burst behind his eyelids like lightning in a thunderstorm, electrifying his body.

This down and dirty sex with Ciara was so completely beyond anything he'd ever experienced with any other woman. His past trysts didn't even compare.

While his mind continued to whirl, his body relaxed, and he found his breath again. He finally released her flesh from his mouth, seeing for the first time the damage he had wrought. From her neck to her shoulder, a dark bruise was already forming.

The wound had to hurt, but he couldn't help but be a little proud of his handiwork, or rather mouthiwork. Teethiwork.

He gently licked the wound and blew a soft puff of healing dragon's breath over the mark he'd made on her. The green mist settled and sank into her skin. The dragon's breath swirled and eddied, instead of relieving the bruises, they concentrated into dark green lines.

Ciara shuddered and her eyes flew open, wiping away the sloppy satisfied smile she had on her face. "What in the world are you doing to me? This must be what they call a whole-body orgasm." Her eyes drifted shut again and she tipped her head to the side exposing her neck and shoulder. The dark lines were forming a shape, but he couldn't quite tell what it was yet.

Her voice was not shocked or scared as he expected, but a low husky sex-laden sound. She moaned again, and the walls of her pussy rhythmically clenched around him again. If his cock thought it was going soft after their joining, it was wrong.

He was as fascinated with her reaction as he was with the magic happening on her skin. He'd done this to her, and she was his to take care of. "Shush, shush. That's it, my sexy, lush witch. Ride that wave of pleasure."

Jakob blew another stream of dragon's breath and enjoyed the first glance of the image before his eyes. The image of an emerald green dragon.

A warmth spread across his body, like being wrapped in a blanket of soft moss. He'd known she was his, and now anyone who looked at her would know too.

Ciara took his command literally and pushed her hips forward, re-seating Jakob's cock fully inside of her. Her feet dug into his ass, holding him exactly where she wanted him.

Her body slid over his again and again driving them both up towards another climax. "Please, Jakob. Please."

Her need pushed at his hunger to have her again. "That's right. Ride my cock, baby."

She slid her eyes open and bit her lip. She ground against him. "It's not enough. Please make me come. Again. Now."

Fucking hell, hearing her try to boss him around was so hot he nearly came inside of her right then. She was a strong, confident, curvy woman, and there was nothing sexier than that.

"You'll do what I say and come when I tell you to, because we both like it when you do." He punctuated his words by pinching her clit again. "You're not in charge here, witch."

She reacted exactly as he hoped she would, hissing in a breath and batting her eyes at him. She wanted to submit, but this gorgeous thing had never found anyone powerful enough to give into.

He would be that man for her. He would be the only man for her.

He released her arms. "Put your hands on my shoulders. Don't let go." She paused the gyration of her hips and stared at him, a flash of rebellion in her eyes. "Do it, Ciara, or you will be left unsatisfied."

She raised an eyebrow, but he caught the sparkle that put in her eye. She did as she was told and gripped his shoulders, digging her fingers and nails into him. Good girl.

With his arms now free, he grabbed her under the knees, forcing her legs into the air.

"Oh, holy yoga," she groaned.

He didn't give her a chance to say another word before he withdrew his aching cock and thrust into her deeper than he'd been before. This new position let him fill her to the hilt. He could stay this way for a day, but that wouldn't get her screaming, pleading to let her come. Which was what they both wanted.

He swiveled his hips, listening to her ragged gasps to find just the right spot. When her yes became nothing more than guttural squeaks, he slowly withdrew, ready to drive her well beyond pleasure.

"Remember, you don't come until I tell you to." He waited for her to nod, gripped the stones around her ass, and slammed his way home, driving into her.

"Oh... oh." Her first exclamation was surprise, but the second was a purr.

Jakob pumped in and out, picking up speed with each of her cries. The grip she had on his shoulders grew tighter and tighter, until he was sure he would have bruises of his own in the morning. The faster he slid in and out of her, the higher her keens.

"Yes. Yes, right there, Jakob. Right there."

The muscles of her channel squeezed and her body shuddered, as she teetered on the brink.

"Ciara, look at me." He was breathing hard and his own body begged for release. But it wouldn't get it until he heard begging from her. He slowed, swiveling his hips again.

She blinked and closed her eyes, not acknowledging anything but the sensations of her body.

"Ciara, look." He sucked in a breath and stopped moving. "At me."

She blinked again and her glazed eyes found him. That's what he wanted to see, her on the verge of losing it, ready to succumb to the pleasure. Because he was about to spike it even higher, make her fly. "Are you allowed to come yet?"

The little reminder that he was still in control had her pussy clenching tighter and she bit her lip.

"Are you?" he growled.

She shook her head.

"Good. Remember that."

He thrust into her one last time and slid out. "Grab on to the side of the phone booth."

He waited for her to obey and then dropped to his knees. He supported her thighs, one in each hand, and spread her wide. Then he flicked his tongue over her clit, lapping up her sweet and salty cream.

She squirmed and jolted, sensitive from all their fucking. "Ooh, Jakob. That is so unfair."

He'd show her unfair. He let one of her legs drop to his shoulder and thrust two fingers into her pussy. He flicked his tongue across her clit, crooked his fingers inside of her, and dragged them across her g-spot. He knew he'd hit it because her moans jumped two octaves.

"What I said earlier about right there, I was wrong. That's the spot." Her breasts heaved with the breaths she took in short pants, showing him she was damn close. He continued to finger her but lifted his mouth. "Don't come."

She whimpered and slammed her head back. He'd never get enough of seeing her like this.

She couldn't have much control left, but he would push it. He continued stroking over her most sensitive places and sucked her clit into his mouth. She squealed and it turned into sobbing gasps.

"Jakob, please. Please."

He knew what she was asking for, but he wouldn't give it to her until she fully begged, said the words. He suckled her clit, flicking his tongue over the sensitive nub inside his mouth.

"Please, please." she squirmed, first trying to pull away from him, and then pushing her plump pussy closer to his mouth.

Not yet.

His own cock was almost as tortured as she was, straining for release. He was as hard as the stones beneath his knees. Harder.

Not yet.

The tremble in her legs became a tremor, and then a full-on quake. The muscles in her ass clenched as she tried to hold back.

Not yet.

"Please, Jakob." She took in a shuddering breath. "Please let me come."

There it was. That's what he'd been waiting for.

He licked her one more time, and stood, not for a second pausing the thrust of his fingers inside of her. Her eyes were screwed shut tight, her little frown clenched between her teeth.

"Ciara, look at me." This time her eyes flew open.

"Please," she moaned.

"Let me hear you say it again. Ask me for it, Ciara. Ask me to let you come."

"Asshat." She panted. "Please let me come."

He chuckled. Even now she had a potty mouth and knew how to use it. He loved that. "That's what I want to hear, my curvy, sexy witch."

He slid his free hand between her pussy lips and flicked his thumb across her clit in time with his fingers inside of her. He bent his head and whispered in her ear. "Come for me, witch. Come now."

Her entire body locked, the final command contracting her muscles. She convulsed with the power of the orgasm. Her pleasure was his, and it was the most beautiful god-damned thing he'd ever seen.

He had every intention of sliding his cock into her and letting her milk him with her heat, come to the pulse of her around him. But she was too hot, and it was too late. He groaned her name and his cock jerked. He came on the stone beneath her ass.

When her body finally released the grip it had on her, she wrapped her arms around his neck and buried her face in his chest.

They were both gasping for breath, floating on cloud nine, ten, and eleven. What the hell kind of sex was that? Sex wasn't even the right word for it.

If anyone was peeping out their windows, Jakob's body would block their view of Ciara. But they had more problems than any voyeurs that might be around. He'd been stupid to allow them to be so exposed and defenseless with the possibility of more demon dragons around.

Man, he was a complete dumbass for letting his instincts outweigh his good judgement. He could have claimed her in the safety of his home, in the comfort of a bed, instead of shoving her up against a metal pole and taking her like the base animal he was.

He would make it up to her. She would have the finest, softest bed, and he would fill her room with every flower in the country. He would make love to her, over and over, repenting with his body for not treating her properly this first time.

He tugged her ripped dress around her thighs and yanked his own pants back on. "Ciara, love. Let me take you home."

She didn't say a word, but let her legs drop and leaned back, pulling away from him. He missed her warmth and her touch immediately.

She pushed his hands away and straightened her clothing herself. The new dragon tattoo shimmered on her neck and shoulder, remaining uncovered by the tatters of her clothing.

The necklace at her throat glimmered, asking him to reach out and touch it. "Is this charm important to you?"

Perhaps he would get a new tattoo to match. He lifted the piece from her neck and the metal disintegrated—no, it shifted, turning into a handful of multi-colored dragon scales.

The First Dragon's relic. It had been right under his nose all along.

The scales swirled as if picked up by a gentle breeze and scattered into the night sky.

Ciara smacked his hand away and grasped for the chain, but it dissolved in her fingers and joined the rest. "Hey, what did you do to my necklace?"

"You did an excellent job hiding it from me. I don't know how you did that. Enough of your games. Bring it back, Ciara. What's yours is mine now."

"What?" The well-loved doe-eyed look vanished from her face.

He should have thought of that before. Sure, he never expected to have a mate. But the human ritual of marriage would have sufficed. If she wouldn't give back what rightfully belonged to him, he'd take it back. If they married, what was hers would also then belong to him.

The AllWyr council would have something to say about

him marrying. The other three Wyr's would be all up in arms about him having mated anyway. Might as well go big.

"Do not go and get all, all, bossy with me, mister." Ciara poked him in the chest.

He'd imagined them walking back to his villa, chatting and holding hands. But he'd gone and pissed her off instead. She was awfully cute all riled up like this.

"But I am bossy. Which you like."

"Ah." She scoffed, but a very pretty shade of pink flashed across her cheeks.

"I didn't do anything to that necklace. I don't even know where I got it."

He searched her eyes, scented the air around her. How could she be telling the truth and lying at the same time? More of her magic.

Soon enough, he'd learn her ways. They were going to spend a lifetime finding out every nook and cranny of each other. He was especially looking forward to licking his way all around those nooks, and especially her cranny.

"Come on, witch of mine. Let's get back before more demon dragons decide they want another taste of you."

Ciara glanced around the empty square, a touch of fear in her eyes. "Didn't you kill them all?"

"Yes, but it's still dark, and more can rise from the shadows until the sun comes up and takes away their powers."

Okay, he didn't actually think any more demon dragons were showing up tonight. But he thoroughly enjoyed the way she bit her lip and grabbed onto his arm.

"Let me fly you back home. Then we'll talk about your necklace, and your powers." In bed.

"We're also talking about why you kidnapped me, and

about… this." She waved her fingers back and forth between them.

"The only talking about this I want to do with you is to find out all about your kinks."

"Oh no. There is something else going on between us, more than the usual lust at first sight stuff. Not to mention whatever you did to my shoulder."

The air in Jakob's mouth and lungs went dry. A mountain of stones piled in his stomach. "Yes. There is."

She didn't know. Of course she didn't. She wasn't Dragonkind.

He'd marked her, claimed her, and she didn't even know what it meant, didn't even know what had happened.

Sex. That's all it was to her.

Except she did know there was more to it, or she wouldn't be pushing at him like this.

How did he explain the magic she'd become for him, a true mate, the one being in the universe who was made especially for him, and him for her?

Ciara yawned, and patted Jakob's cheek. "Don't drop me this time."

Jakob was the one who felt like he'd been dropped. On his head. Or maybe his heart.

WHAT HAD SHE DONE?

Ciara let Jakob fly her back to his villa, because what else was she supposed to do?

A crazy white witch had taught her magic, black snake people had tried to eat her, and then Jakob had.

Eaten her, that is.

She blushed in places she didn't even know she could, simply thinking about Jakob between her legs and inside her.

It had been...wow. Absolutely fucking amazeballs.

How was he still single with skills like that? Oh, God. Maybe he wasn't.

Shit. She wasn't. In the inferno of the moment, she'd forgotten all about Wes. Jakob's kisses, and licks, and bites had obliterated Wes from her mind.

What had she done? The guilt of having cheated on him chomped on her core like a hungry hungry hippo.

But wait.

Had she cheated? She didn't actually have a relationship with Wes. They hadn't even gone out on a date yet.

Sure, in her head for the last three years, they'd been

married with kids. But in real life, they were nothing more than coworkers.

He certainly didn't seem to be missing her. Didn't even know she was gone. Sure sounded like he'd been out partying with his friends. Bros before hoes, she guessed.

That phrase summed up every relationship she'd ever had.

Probably because her life was mostly fries before guys.

Now she'd gone and had some serious sexy times with a man - dragon - whatever, who had kidnapped her, saved her from come-to-life nightmare monsters, and she'd liked it.

A lot.

Fuck my life.

Ciara had gone so far inside her head, she didn't even notice they were coming in for a landing at the villa until Jakob popped into her head.

Want to go for another roll in the hay, love?

"Don't even think about it."

I'm definitely thinking about it, and all the other ways I'd like to roll around with you.

While she could think of at least fourteen different positions she'd like to try with him, there would not be any more sexy times until they talked.

Jakob swooped down and gently set Ciara on the grass, far from any of the black stains scattered over the ground. He landed next to her and the dragon form shimmered, fading like a mirage, until only the man stood in front of her.

He touched her cheek, stroking across her chin. "Come on. Let's get you covered up and find something to eat. You must be starving."

She should be offended, because that's what girls with big butts and bellies were when a guy offered them food. Even if she were starving, she'd never eat anything more than chicken breast and a salad on a date.

Sigh. This wasn't a date.

Screw salad. Salad was for sissies.

She was hungry. She could eat a cow, as long as it had cheese and mayo on it.

Besides, this was the second time Jakob had tried to feed her. He didn't seem to care that she had some extra cushion. In fact, he'd liked it pretty damn well when he'd been pushing against that cushion a half-hour ago.

"I could eat."

Jakob smiled and she saw all the dirty thoughts her words sent through his mind. He took her hand and dragged her through the courtyard and into the house. She would protest his caveman-like behavior, but she had a brilliant view of his butt.

What a fine butt it was too.

She could think of so many very fun things to do with that butt.

Not to mention all the dirty things she'd like him to do to her butt.

Geez, horny much?

She was doing exactly what she always did when she first got into a relationship with the new guy. Not that that had happened a whole lot, but this was her M. O. Skip the important bits like whether they had anything in common or were even compatible, and instead went straight into fantasyland.

It wasn't like she was even in a relationship with Jakob. They'd had sex.

Fucking fantastic sex, but this didn't even yet count as a one-night stand.

She never should have let it go that far. So he had shown

more interest in her than Wes or any other man she'd ever dated. Or not dated. Didn't mean they were going to live happily ever after.

Even though she let her imagination run all the way up the aisle, it wasn't like her to just jump into bed—or jump into a phone booth—with a guy she had only met yesterday.

Met wasn't even accurate. He kidnapped her. And then she'd gone and slept with him.

What the holy cannolis?

Her emotions were completely out of whack, and that was affecting her judgment. It had to be this place. She knew better.

Emotions made one do dumb and stupid things, like sleep with a dragon.

The white witch, formerly known as Mrs. Bohacek, had warned her that suppressing her emotions, like she had grown up doing her entire life, would burn down the house. She had already almost burned up Jakob's treasure trove.

There was a difference between suppressing one's emotions and keeping a calm and clear mind. That wasn't the same thing. Not at all. Not even close.

Okay then, she would calmly and clearly eat and then tell Jakob thanks, but no thanks. She wanted to go home. They were beyond kidnapper and kidnappee now. They could have an adult conversation at last.

She never had his whosie-whatsie in the first place, and he would understand that now.

He would fly her home. Or maybe she would take a few more days off and spend them in Prague. Not like anyone had missed her anyway. Not like she had anyone to go home to.

She could go home next week to her sad and pathetic life lusting after a man who didn't even want her, and working ninety hours a week for her mother helping other people get their happy ever afters.

Yeah. Good plan.

Jakob whistled as he guided her through the house to the kitchen. Of course he did. He was a dude who just got laid.

With no strings attached.

He snagged a soft green throw off a chair they passed and stopped long enough to wrap it around her like a shawl. His fingers rubbed over the place between her neck and shoulder where he'd bitten her.

Who would have thought she'd be into biting? But when he'd dug his teeth into her, man oh man, how her body had said 'hell yeah.'

"You won't be wearing any of this long, but I promise to get you all the most beautiful clothes in the world if you want them. Except for panties. No panties. Ever."

She didn't know what to say to that. No man had ever offered to buy her clothes. She didn't need him to anyway. She had a closet stuffed to overflowing at home. Where she would be tomorrow.

Ciara opened her mouth to say as much, but her stomach growled, or maybe it was her psyche. Either way a cheeseburger would do wonders. They could talk afterwards.

He bopped her on the nose. For real. Like something an adorable couple would do.

They were not a couple. They never would be.

"Come on, let's see what kind of meal we can whip up. We'll need our strength."

He winked at her and brushed his lips across hers.

She wished he wouldn't do that. It made it hard to keep that calm and clear mind.

Jakob smacked her on the butt and then put his hand on

the small of her back, guiding her to the kitchen. Every tingle she'd ever had in her entire life was nothing compared to the buzzy bees tickling her right where Jakob's hand rested.

They walked into the kitchen, but Jakob stopped short, just inside the entry way. He moved like The Flash and jumped in front of her. Ciara squeaked, expecting another attack from the snake people. None came.

She tentatively peeked around him to see what other kind of scary monster might be in the kitchen.

A man leaned against the counter, arms folded, like he didn't have a care in the world. Except there was something about the way his eyes were on alert, going to her face and then Jakob's face. He wasn't relaxed, even a little bit.

Neither was Jakob. He squeezed her hand and did his best to block her view of the visitor.

The other man spoke first. "Hello, brother. How are the winds treating you this fine night?"

Ciara looked between the two men standing off. Neither seemed angry, more like territorial. Where Jakob made her heart go pitter-patter-what's-the-matter with his dark hair, that yummy stubble on his chin, and bright green eyes, his brother was a blond god with golden eyes. They looked nothing alike. Brothers from another mother, maybe. "This is your brother?"

Jakob didn't move, because he'd lose the staring contest then. "Not exactly. He's another Wyvern. Leader of the Gold Dragons."

"Oh." Huh. She'd just assumed dragons were all green since that's what Jakob was. What was she saying? All dragons? Up until yesterday the only dragon she knew of was Puff. There was one more question on her list for when she and Jakob had that talk.

Ciara moved around her incredible hulk of a dragon and stretched out her hand, careful to keep the blanket covering the tatters of her dress. No need for more than one dragon to see her half-naked tonight. "Nice to meet you. I'm Ciara Mosley-Willingham."

He straightened up and took her hand, his fingertips dancing over her pulse point. "The pleasure is entirely mine, beauty. You can call me Cage."

A low rumbling growl came from behind her and this time it wasn't anyone's stomach.

Cage raised his hands in the air and stepped back, but with a flirty grin on his face.

"My apologies, greenie. I didn't know you were—" he paused, tilted his head, and inhaled through his nose. "That's very interesting."

Jakob stuck his arms out, soccer mom style, blocking her from Cage. She stuck her head out from under his arm anyway. "What is?"

Cage sniffed the air again and narrowed his eyes. "Your scents. They're—"

Jakob pushed Ciara back behind him, blocking both her view and Cage's words. "What are you doing here, Cage?"

"I came to see what the fuss with my golds over the Atlantic Ocean was the other night. I hear you took a flight."

"I did."

Cage looked between Jakob and Ciara, trying to work something out. Was it completely obvious they'd slept together, like a half an hour ago?

Crap. He could smell it, couldn't he? She was investing in Febreeze.

"Must have been pretty important if you couldn't talk to me about the flight over. That's a long trip for a green."

"It was, and it was." Jakob was being incredibly tight-lipped about whatever these two were talking about.

"I see that." Cage waggled his eyes at Ciara while he looked her up and down in a way that made her giggle. What a charmer.

Jakob had some macho protective mojo going on, but nothing but curiosity and friendliness came from Cage.

Yep. She could tell that. It wasn't a guess, she wasn't paying attention to his body language to come to that conclusion. She knew it.

Cage might be a looker, but Jakob was the one she'd gotten down and dirty with. The one she'd like to get even dirtier with.

Ugh. No, she was leaving. She'd decided. Regardless, she didn't want to see some kind of man war between these two because Jakob was going all feral on her.

She put her hand on Jakob's arm, thinking her touch might calm him. It worked with brides and grooms and fathers of the brides, and mothers of the grooms. She literally felt the muscles in his arms relax under her hand.

He finally looked at her, quirked and eyebrow up for a second, and they took a deep breath together.

"Dude. Who is this sexy chick?" Cage's voice had an aura of awe in it.

Jakob didn't respond but searched her eyes. She sensed another emotion from him now. Regret? No, that wasn't quite right. There was something he was holding back, something he wasn't telling her.

His pendant turned on, like an old TV warming up, very faint at first, like its light was only meant for her to see.

"She's my...guest."

"A guest who makes your soul shard glow? She's more than a guest, Zeleny. What the fuck is going on here?"

"Ciara is no ordinary human. She had the First Dragon's relic."

Oh boy, not this again. "I never took your First Dragon's anything."

Maybe she'd been wrong about him understanding that now.

"Holy shit, dude. You got it back from her, didn't you?" Cage began pacing back and forth from the sink to the refrigerator in a circle.

"No. It's gone." Jakob's entire attitude was different. He didn't seem quite so worked up as he had every other time they had talked about this relic. Could she have possibly have done that? The elements and her emotions were obviously intertwined, because she had to use them to affect the fire, wind, and earth. She hadn't yet tried anything with water.

It made sense that if she learned to control the elements, that she might also be able to do something with emotions. She had always been really good at calming people down. It was half of what made her good at her job.

A job she was probably going to lose. That thought didn't hurt as much as it should.

Her job was her life. She should be freaking out right now. Not so much.

"Gone? Gone where? You've got to get it back. That's the job of the Green Dragon Wyvern. Your Wyr was the one entrusted to watch over the relic. You can't just fucking lose it." Cage had added a lot of gesticulations with his pacing. He was getting really worked up.

Ciara took a quiet breath and concentrated on Cage. In her mind's eye she thought of a pretty green field with a quiet blue sky dotted with only a few puffy clouds here and there. Sunshine warmed the air and birds twittered in her head.

Cage stopped and stretched his back and shoulders. He glanced over at Ciara and his jaw dropped open.

"Did you do that?"

"Maybe. Do you feel better?"

"I'm having a cow. But it sure as hell doesn't feel like it." Cage grinned and flashed her one of those smiles you see in toothpaste commercials. If life had a soundtrack the sparkle of his smile would have dinged.

"Why don't you tell us what you did with the relic?"

Ciara raised her hands and took a step back. Now she had to convince both of them. Great.

"I don't think Ciara had anything to do with the theft." Jakob sidled up next to her and put his hand on the small of her back again. She couldn't think straight when he did that. Bastard.

No way he had just said she didn't steal his thingamabob.

"After the attack on us both tonight and the aftermath," the only indication Jakob gave about said aftermath was the tiniest crinkle next to his eyes. "I think whoever stole the relic planted it so that I would find her."

What?

"Besides the fact she has some very interesting powers, what makes her special, important? Why would anyone risk the First Dragon's relic to bring her to you?

Oh yeah, because she loved being talked about as if she wasn't standing right there. "Hello?" She waved her hands to remind the two men she was not an inanimate object.

"Sorry, kitten." Cage had enough sense to look abashed at his bad behavior.

Jakob swirled his thumb in a circle on her back. She didn't

want him to do that, but she didn't want him to stop either, so she didn't say anything.

"Her powers are extraordinary. I've never seen anything like it. She commands three out of the four elements without so much as a twitch of her nose. But that wouldn't bring a horde of fifty or so demon dragons down on us."

Cage nodded. "I saw the black marks in your garden. I assume your troops took care of them."

"No, I sent them away yesterday. All but Steele, who is now en route to the US."

"You're telling me you and kitten here defeated fifty demon dragons."

"That's what you call those black snake people?" Demon dragons? That sounded a hell of a lot worse than snake people. Were they demons, or dragons, or both? Jakob cleared his throat and Ciara giggled to herself over the way his chest puffed up. "I took care of them."

"Yeah, right. Not unless you found a way to quadruple your powers." Cage scoffed at Jakob and jerked his thumb at him. He grinned at Ciara like they had some sort of conspiratorial agreement that Jakob was a dumbass.

Ciara stuck her tongue out at him.

"As soon as the sun rises and I'm sure Ciara is safe, we can take this outside and I'll show you."

Great. The dragons were going to get their dicks out and measure them.

"Sounds fun. But we'd better save it for the AllWyr Council." Cage leaned back against the counter. "Have fun explaining to Match how you lost the First Dragon's relic to meet a hot chick."

"I've got a lot more to tell the AllWyr Council about." Jakob chucked Ciara on the chin and moved the blanket from her right shoulder, exposing it to Cage's view.

Cage's jaw not only dropped open again, but his eyeballs about popped out of his head.

What? What did he see? Ciara twisted her head to look at herself but could only see someone's shoulder. There was no way that that was her skin because she did not have a giant tattoo of a green dragon.

"Like the fact that Ciara is my true soulmate and that I have claimed her."

Those tingles that Jakob put in her back traveled up her spine, pinged her in the back of the skull, and sent pins and needles across her scalp.

This was going to throw a kink in her plans. Not the kind of kink that got her motor running, the kind that stopped it dead.

YOU BELONG TO ME

*I*f Ciara hadn't worked some sort of magic on all of their emotions, Cage's head would have exploded. Into a million pieces.

Jakob knew exactly how he felt.

But he was less concerned about Cage's reaction to his declaration as he waited to see what Ciara did.

So far, she hadn't moved a muscle. Seriously, she was frozen.

"Ciara, honey?" He'd take anything from her at the moment. Tears, anger, she could even slap him in the face.

Mating was a pretty big thing to spring on a person, even if she didn't fully understand the extent of what a dragon's true mate meant.

She did none of those things. Instead, she pushed his arm away and walked out of the kitchen.

Shit. That was probably bad.

He followed her, and Cage was hot on his heels. She went back through the great room and up the stairs, moving fast enough that he had to take them two at a time just to catch up.

"Ciara, talk to me."

She held up a hand, and then just one finger. That finger shook at him, but Ciara still didn't say anything. She kept walking until she got to the guest room he'd put her in yesterday.

Was it all too much for her? Was she going to collapse? Go to bed and pulled the covers over her head? Christ, he'd done this to her. Broken his mate when it was his job to protect her, keep her safe.

It wasn't like he could ask any other dragons for their advice on how to handle a mate. No one else had a mate or even thought they would. He was making this up as he went along.

If he had to wrap her up in cotton—or even better cotton candy—he would protect her, make her feel safe.

She threw the door open and went to stand in front of a dresser that had a small mirror hanging on the wall over it.

The blanket covering her fell to the floor and she bared her shoulder.

The reflection staring back at her was confused. Lips pressed together into a thin line, and wide eyes that watched her fingers brush over the mark he'd given her. The dragon sparkled under her touch.

"What. The. Hell. Is. This?"

Okay. She was pissed. He could handle that. At least now he knew what he was dealing with.

"She's gonna kick your ass, man." Cage whispered, having way too much fun over this. Any second now he was going to pull up a chair and grab some popcorn.

"Fuck off."

"Nope."

Jakob could only hope that someday Cage would find a

mate too. Mostly so that Jakob could make Cage's life just as miserable when that happened.

He didn't even know if that was likely. He knew nothing about how or why he'd been blessed with Ciara.

"Jakob," she snarled.

Cage was right. She was pissed. Cute as hell too. Her cheeks had that same flush to them when she was mad as when she was coming.

All Jakob wanted to do was take Ciara to bed and show her exactly what that mark meant. "Cage, get out."

Ciara pointed to Cage. "Oh no. If you won't tell me what you did to me, then maybe he will."

Cage held up his hands and began to back out of the room. He was no dumb dragon.

"This doesn't concern him. That mark is between you and me."

"This isn't a mark. This is unauthorized body art. It's a frickin' tattoo."

Cage made it to the door, and grabbed the handle to pull it shut, leaving Jakob and Ciara alone. "She's gonna kill you. But if you survive this, you've got to call an AllWyr ASAP. Have fun with that."

Cage shut the door, leaving that little truth bomb to explode inside Jakob's head.

Shit.

He could call an AllWyr, a meeting of all four Wyverns, and then everyone would see how he fucked up. He certainly wasn't turning out to be the leader his father had been. But what choice did he have?

The villa and his lair had been compromised, demon dragons had tried to steal his soul shard, and he had marked and claimed a mate.

He was in way over his head. He'd been trained to lead his troops in battle against evil and keep peace among his Wyr.

That's what his father and his father's father before him had done. It's what all Wyverns had done since the first great battle a couple thousand years ago. If that's all he had to do, he'd be a bad ass Wyvern.

But mating? Love?

He had no idea when it came to either of them.

He'd known Ciara for a couple of days, there wasn't time for love. This mating was completely instinctual, it had very little to do with feelings.

"Is there any way to get this thing off of me? Why would you put a tattoo on me in the first place?" Ciara rubbed her fingers over the mark like she was trying to rub it off.

He might be feeling like a failure at the moment, but he needed to put that aside and take care of his mate, which was something he hadn't done since the second he'd found her.

Jakob finally figured out how to pull his head out of his ass and crossed the room to Ciara. He placed his hand over hers and stopped her scrubbing at the mark.

"A lot has happened in the past few days and quite honestly it's as overwhelming to me as I think it is for you."

She glanced at him in the mirror, a flash of mixed emotions flew through her eyes staring back at him. There was a good dose of disbelief, some frustration, and the one that bothered him the most, fear. He'd done more than enough to make her fear him. The opposite of what a mate should be doing. He needed to start earning her trust instead.

"I am sorry for everything I've put you through. But I won't apologize for claiming you. I will be thanking the First Dragon for the rest of my life that we were brought together."

Ciara's shoulders sagged under his hand. "I'm not your property to claim."

She tried to jerk away, but he didn't want her to think he was some misogynistic pig. He couldn't blame her. He been acting like a dick, hulking over her, controlling her every move. What could he do to show her what he meant?

Jakob grasped both of her hands in his and sank down to his knees in front of her. "It's not like that."

She looked down at him, pretty eyes wide. "Really?" Some snowflakes formed a halo around her head. "You don't think I belong to you now?"

There was frost in her voice, but she'd tempered it. The snow dissipated before it even hit her hair. He hoped it was his actions that had done that, and not her suppressing her emotions again. He swallowed, trying to choose his next words very carefully.

He was either in for a flurry of kisses or a smackdown of snow.

"I do. You do belong to me, but I belong to you too. We were made for each other."

She shook her head. "No, I don't see how that could be at all."

Humans believed in the concept of soulmates. There were enough sappy books and movies to prove that. But the human mating ritual was nothing like that of dragons. They danced around each other. Dragons marked, claimed, and mated. He needed to find an in-between for his mate. "You're my true soulmate. We were destined to be together."

Her brow furrowed, making a cute little crinkle. "I've seen too many happy couples in my line of work to not believe in destiny. But how do you know?"

Good question. It wasn't like he had a manual on mating.

"I'm operating completely on instinct with you. Every cell inside of me, every scale on my body knows that you are mine."

"I could maybe accept that if we'd known each other for years, and dated, and...well I was gonna say had sex, but we did do that part."

"We did that part really well." The next time would be even better.

Her eyes softened, and one side of her mouth lifted in a partial grin. He was making progress.

"Could we do those other things? The getting to know each other and dating? Or do I have some horrible form of that syndrome, you know, the one where the hostage falls in love with her kidnapper? I really don't understand how I could possibly not hate you. But I don't, and that's weird to me."

He would love to romance her. He would buy her a new beautiful green gown and white gloves, choose a diamond necklace from his treasure, and fly her to Prague, where they would see an opera like La Traviata. She would probably like it better than the Pirates of Penzance. Unfortunately, with the demon dragon attack and his suspicions about what had really happened to the relic, there would be no time for wining and dining her.

"I would love nothing more, but I don't think our situation will allow that."

She stepped away from him, trying to hide her disappointment.

That shredded his heart, and he swore to someday make it up to her.

Right now, he had a choice to make. No, this choice he needed to allow her to be in charge. He got back to his feet and stood behind her, wanting her to feel his presence, but not touching her.

"If you want me to take you back to your home in America, I will." Even if it would kill him.

"I have a whole life to get back to there. I have a date on Thursday with Wesley." Ciara licked her lips and made a face like she had a bad taste in her mouth.

Over his dead body. He wouldn't yet tell her that if she refused him, there would be no other for either of them. He didn't want that to influence her decision that way. "Stay."

She didn't say anything, which punched him in the gut. Now was the time to push his case. He knew she felt something for him, he'd scent it on her if she didn't. Maybe presenting her with the rest of his working theory would help persuade her.

"There's something more going on besides you and I mating. The massive attack of the demon dragons here at the villa, the attempt to steal my soul shard, and to get to you are all connected somehow."

She paced back and forth. He tracked every step. "I wouldn't be safe if I went back home, would I?"

"I would send an entire battalion of green dragon warriors to guard you."

"But you wouldn't be there."

If she wanted to be his mate, they would have to be here, in his homeland, where his people and his Wyr were. "No."

"I figured. My life is never going to be the same, is it?" She didn't sound as bothered by that statement as he'd thought she would be.

"No. The mating changes things." If he were very, very lucky, it would be for the better for them both.

"Yeah, you're going to have to give me the mating 101, or at least the Cliff's notes."

Her statement gave him hope that she was considering being with him. He'd happily spend the rest of his life teaching her about mating. She'd be teaching him too.

"I haven't exactly been safe here either. Are those demon dudes after you or me?"

"I will do everything in my power to keep you safe. I don't think they were after me exactly. One of them tried to steal my soul shard. They may have been after your necklace."

"I don't even know what it was or where it came from."

He had a theory about that. "I think someone took the First Dragon's relic and planted it on you in the form of that necklace. It had some powerful spells on it though because until I touched it, I had no idea what it was either."

She stopped her pacing. "You don't think I'm a thief anymore?"

She'd tried to tell him all along, but he hadn't listened. "No. Whoever took the relic from my lair wanted me to find you. They knew you were my mate."

No dragon had that kind of power, no human either. Another kind of demon maybe? Not a demon dragon, there weren't the sharpest tools in the shed. Succubi and Incubi traded in sex and blood, not souls. Nothing in his knowledge had the kind of power to change the fate of dragons.

"But if we we're destined to be together, like you say, wouldn't you have eventually found me anyway? Or couldn't I find you?"

Dragons had been searching for the cure for their lack of mates for centuries. They'd mostly given up hope.

"I don't think so. No dragon in the last seven hundred

years has found his mate. Or if he did, he didn't know she was the one. I never imagined you were even out there for me."

He still hardly believed it, except when he looked at her and felt it all the way from his scales to his bones that they belonged together.

"Seven hundred years seems like a long time for a race to be without husbands or wives."

"Wives isn't exactly the right word for a dragon warrior's mate, but close enough since all of them are female."

"Lesbian dragons?"

That made Jakob laugh out loud. "No, although there are some gay dragons, so I guess every mate isn't a woman. But there is no such thing as a female dragon."

"Really?"

"Yes, we are all sons of the First Dragon. I am the first son of the first son of the first son, etcetera, of the first green dragon."

"That's a lot of sons for not having any mothers."

"The past few generations of mateless dragons have had companions." He'd ignored the fact that his Prime had crept up on him and he'd soon be expected to take a companion. No woman had interested him lately. Then bam.

"Like Dr. Who?"

"No. Some companions are like wives, some are not. But they are all lovers. Many are mothers of dragons."

"Oh, I see. You're all a bunch of dragon man whores."

He supposed they were. The fifty years between when he hit puberty and the beginning of his Prime, he'd been one horny fucker. But until his father's death, he hadn't ever considered having a son. Until right this moment, because having a child with Ciara had just zipped up to the top of his priority list. His dick woke right up at the thought of seeing her ripe and pregnant with his younglings.

Unless, of course, she chose to leave.

"Most companions are very special to their dragons." Ciara was much too far away. He carefully stalked toward her. "I suspect if we hadn't lost the ability to mate, many of them would have marked and claimed their women, just as I have you." She saw him coming and skittered to the other side of the big bed in the room. That was fine, he would more than happily pull her onto it.

She wasn't really trying to get away from him, but his instincts pushed him to chase her.

"If I decided I didn't want to go back to America right now," she held up her hands to stop his forward progress, "do you have someone like that Mrs. Bohacek woman, who can help me learn how to use these crazy ass powers I seem to have manifested?"

"You mentioned her before, my little dumpling, but I still don't know who you're talking about."

He placed one knee on the bed and planted the ball of his foot into the floor, ready to spring if she bolted. She snagged a pillow off the bed and held it out in front of her. Like that would stop him.

"You must. She knows you, was in your house, was even in your lair. You know, real beautiful, long white flowing dress, has more magic than a fairy godmother."

Jakob pushed a tiny portion of his shift to his back and prepared to unfurl his wings. But her comment about being in his lair stopped him.

"Where else did you see this woman?"

"She came to me here right after you locked me in the room and took me down to the kitchen. I thought she was

going to help me escape but then she said something strange
—"

She didn't finish her sentence, but her expression changed
to surprise and then she threw a pillow at him. He blocked it
and tossed it aside.

"What did she say, Ciara?" He pounced off the bed and
missed her by a scant centimeter. A puff of wind pushed him
back.

"Nothing." She scrunched up her nose and the fireplace
reignited. "Shoot, that's not what I meant to do."

"What did she say, Ciara?" Jakob used his own magic and
brought the potted plants in the corner of the room to life.
While she wasn't looking he grew them to the ceiling.

He feinted to the left making her go right. Right where he
wanted her.

She scrambled toward the headboard. "That's between me
and her."

This time when she jumped, he was ready. The vines
dropped from the ceiling snagging her around the waist,
shoulders, and legs. They dragged her into the air, suspending
her, and she squealed.

"That's not fair. I don't know how to talk plants into doing
my dirty work."

Jakob took advantage of her position and slid his hand up
her thigh. God how he'd missed touching her for the whole
time they'd been talking. He would not be keeping his hands,
or his lips to himself any longer. "They won't be doing all of
my dirty work. I save the dirtiest for myself."

She wiggled, not budging the vines, but making her ass
jiggle enough to put his cock on high alert. "You let me down,
you pervert."

She had no idea.

He continued to trace his hand up past her hip, into that luscious curve at her waist and up her ribcage. "You like it when I'm perverted."

She huffed, or was that a stifled giggle? "That's not the point."

She made him laugh, she made him more powerful, she made him want to be a better man, a better dragon. She couldn't leave.

He adjusted the vines so her head fell back, face to face with him. She was breathing heavy, lips parted, eyes dilated.

Hot damn, she'd enjoyed the chase and being caught as much as he had, and they'd barely played the game. It would be so much more satisfying to get her out into the forest around the villa.

She could run, but she couldn't hide from him.

He wanted to kiss her, take her, claim her all over again. In this position, she'd be at his mercy. He could do anything he pleased, and he had no doubt that she'd love it.

If she truly didn't want to stay, he wouldn't make her. It would be too hard to have her again now, knowing he had to give her up.

"Ciara." God, his voice was husky with needing her.

"Yes?" she whispered.

"Stay with me."

Once again, she didn't respond. He traced a finger over her lips, practically begging for her yes. She still needed convincing.

"I can only help you understand the magic of the earth element, but the other Wyverns can help you learn to control the fire and wind the way you want to."

Her tongue darted out of her mouth, teasing his finger. "Tempting. Let me down and we can talk about it."

As enticing as she was suspended before him, he couldn't lie to himself and say that was the only reason he'd tied her up this way. Here, she couldn't get away from him, couldn't avoid making the decision.

He needed to know now, even if he forced her into choosing.

Jakob leaned down, placing his lips a breath away from hers. "Neither of us will ever be the same if you leave."

She blew out a soft breath. "I'll never be the same again anyway."

"What can I say to convince you?"

"Please."

What a dick. This whole time he'd demanded from her while telling himself the choice was up to her.

"Ciara. Please stay with me. I want very little more from the rest of my life but to keep you safe and revel in the delights of your body."

For an instant those emotions he'd seen flashing through her before, frustration and fear were back. He'd done something wrong. Fuck.

A second before he dropped to his knees again, to beg her with all that he had, she whispered the one word he wanted to hear.

"Yes."

The vines unrolled and set her in his arms. He took her mouth in a crushing kiss, punishing her for making him wait so damn long to taste her again.

She gave as good as she got, biting his lip and sucking it into his mouth. He was going to fuck her until neither of them could see straight, and then he was going to do it all over again.

A knock sounded at the door, which he completely

ignored. He pushed Ciara toward the bed, insistent on taking her somewhere a hell of a lot softer than stones this time.

The knock came again, this time louder and in a continuous rap. "If you two are done making up in there, we've got company."

"Fuck off." There was no way anyone was more important than getting inside Ciara and making her come at least a half dozen times.

"Sounds like fun, but I think you're going to want to come down here."

"My dragon said fuck off."

Her potty mouth was hot as hell.

The door blasted off its hinges and blew across the room. Ciara squeaked and jumped behind him. The vines he'd been playing with dropped from the ceiling and ensconced Cage and two other dragons almost instantly.

He hadn't done that. Ciara peeked around his back and the vines grew a whole host of new leaves.

"I thought you said you didn't know how to command plants."

"I panicked, and it just happened."

"Get me the fuck out of your trap, Jakob Zeleny, or I'll burn every plant in this house down."

Well, shit. Match Cervony, Red Wyvern and alpha of alphas was hanging like a firefly in a spiderweb a meter from the ceiling.

"Not my trap. If you want out, I suggest you ask nicely. It works wonders with the ladies."

"Pretty wahine, let me down and I'll water your plants for you." Ky Puru, the Blue Dragon Wyvern was already fucking flirting with Ciara.

Jakob, being the youngest and newest Wyvern, rarely had

an opportunity this ripe. He wouldn't have it for long, so he was taking advantage of it.

"Gentleman, while we've got your full attention, I'd like you all to meet Ciara. My mate."

All three Wyverns dropped from the ceiling into a heap on the carpet.

"Oops. My bad," Ciara said from behind him.

God, he loved her already.

Oh shit. He did. He loved her.

ALLWYR OR ALL WEIRD?

*O*nce the three dragons had unraveled themselves from Ciara's accidental plant trap, she saw how big and intimidating the other males were. Not that they were any bigger than Jakob, but the one they called Match was so grumpy like a grizzly bear that he seemed a lot bigger than he was.

Where Cage was built like a lithe muscular soccer player, Ky had that rough rugby player air about him, not to mention his dark skin and tribal tattoos. Cage and Ky were flirty and welcoming, Match was cranky and broody.

The four of them were currently in the middle of a heated discussion on whether fifty demon dragons constituted a pack or a horde. They traipsed outside to the garden and field where Jakob had battled those monsters, dragging her along.

The black stains on the ground were beginning to fade, and the ashy residue either combined with the dirt or blew away in the breeze.

This sight was part of why Ciara had agreed to stay with Jakob. For now. There was no way she could risk bringing the demon dragons back to America where they would be able to attack her family and friends, who really were just her colleagues. It was horrible of her to imagine her mother running screaming from a snakelike creature in her pristine house, right?

There was another part of her that wanted to be here with him. Wanted badly to believe his story about destiny and being his mate.

It was the same part that had held out for him to ask her to stay instead of ordering her to. Stupid hopeless romantic.

She knew better than to act that way. But it had worked. He'd asked her, and she couldn't say no.

There had to be some batshit crazy in her belfries.

Who decided to shack up with a kidnapping warrior dragon?

Her, that's who.

She wasn't sure now if she should head straight to pathetics anonymous or hit the wedding registry.

Maybe both.

The sun was burgeoning on the horizon, and the shadows where Ciara was sure the demons were hiding, rapidly shrank. Not that she thought Jakob or the other burly warriors would let anything happen to her. He hadn't even let go of her hand since the other dragons had shown up. Besides, she knew better now how to defend herself against paranormal creatures.

Magic.

She even sounded crazypants to herself inside of her own damn head.

Match grumbled something, and the group gathered back inside the house near the secret entrance to Jakob's lair. She felt his uncomfortableness with their proximity to his hiding spot. She didn't know much about dragons, but if there was any truth in the stories and fairy tales, a dragon's treasure was a closely guarded secret.

"If the relic is gone, and your supposed mate didn't take it, then we need to assess the problem with your security." Match sure was being bossy. "We can't risk losing any other dragon lore from your lair. Just show us where it is."

"I've already got Steele working on the problem." Jakob's hand squeezed and released Ciara's like a pulse. Poor guy was going to turn her hand to pulp.

She could tell them about how Mrs. Bohacek just appeared, but none of them were really listening to her anyway. They were way wrapped up in being alphaholes.

They continued to work out their own problems, while she tried to figure out what she was going to tell her mother about not coming home. She hadn't had a vacation in forever, she was due. She'd simply just have to call and say she was taking an extended leave of absence. Wes could take care of most of her accounts anyway. He had a real knack with the brides. It was that million-dollar smile and the panty melting wink he had.

Even Ciara had fallen for it.

Maybe she'd just email her mother. Avoid the drama llama.

But what was she going to say to Wes? Sorry about our date, and hope you had fun at the club the other night?

Yeah, that didn't sound bitter or anything.

If anything, he would be the one who deserved to be upset. She was about to break their first date because she was mated to a dragon.

Not like she could tell Wes that. She didn't even know if he would be bummed out.

All she'd ever done was make assumptions about how he,

and really everyone around her, felt. She never asked. Maybe he didn't even like her that way. On the other hand, she'd spent the last three years around eighty percent sure she was in love with him, so it hurt to think that he might not have shared any of those feelings.

What did she know about love anyway?

She knew what it looked like, on other people anyway. She should have a clue how it really felt.

She glanced at Jakob who was scowling at the other three dragon warriors. He was so damn handsome. But she wanted to rub those worry wrinkles around his eyes away for him.

She shook her head at herself. He made her feel things, pulled up emotions she thought long dead. Emotions she had never been taught to use in the first place.

Was that really her—her feelings? Or was it this bizarre mating thing? Jakob had said he simply knew she was his mate. Maybe those instincts he had talked about were impacting her too.

It could be like when certain animals went into heat. They were drawn to find a mate and reproduce.

Aww, wouldn't a tiny green-eyed version of Jakob running around underfoot be simply adorable?

Kids had never been a part of her relationship equation before. Wesley would probably make beautiful babies too, but she felt nothing when thinking about having his offspring.

It had to be the mating thing. She really needed some time alone with Jakob, not in a bedroom or a phone booth, to find out more about her psychological and physical responses.

Biology. It was all about biology.

It had nothing to do with love.

Gulp.

They were already mated according to Jakob, so she didn't need to worry about things like love.

Because she was not in love with him. Ridiculous.

Except, what if she was?

If love felt anything like longing and deep unfulfilled needs, then she was screwed.

"I am not showing you where my lair is. That is final, so fuck off Match."

Whew, tensions were getting out of control. She could probably do something about that, if she weren't so damn hungry.

Huh. She'd been in Jakob's kitchen three or four times since she'd been here and hadn't yet had anything to eat. No wonder she was running out of steam.

Ciara held a hand up in the middle of the group and swirled a little wind around for emphasis. Cage smiled at her and Jakob stepped closer. Match and Ky both watched her like she was a sideshow attraction.

"Let's take this into the kitchen and discuss this like adults and grown-up dragons over breakfast." She didn't wait for their response and walked away, dragging Jakob along with her since he still hadn't released her hand.

Mr. Grumpypants back there grumbled, but she heard him following them. The men moved to sit around the island, like she was going to wait on them.

She rooted through the refrigerator and found eggs and a tray of leftover cooked bacon. Rock on.

She found forks and a couple of large bowls next. Then set them in front of Ky and Cage. She slid the container of eggs over to Match "I would like five eggs cracked into that bowl, please."

Match stared at her for a minute and raised one eyebrow

when she didn't flinch under his gaze. She smacked her lips and folded her arms. "If you would like to eat breakfast, you're going to have to help prepare it. I may be a mate, but I am not a slave."

Cage and Ky made that oh-ho laughing sound guys did when one of their crew got told.

Ciara kept herself from grinning and turned her back on the group. A moment later, she heard eggs being cracked, followed by the sound of whisking with a fork.

"What would you like my help with, badass? I mean mate." It tickled her that Jakob liked her for making his grumpy friend help with breakfast.

"Can you find me a loaf of bread please?"

She had French toast frying in a big ole cast-iron skillet with gobs of butter just a few minutes later. She threw the bacon in the oven to warm.

In a few more minutes, she had French toast fried egg and bacon sandwiches ready for everyone. As soon the guys bit into their sandwiches, the tension between them slipped away. Amazing what a little food could do. Plus, she had concentrated on imbuing the food with a sense of calm, just to see if she could.

She grabbed the dishes and put them in the sink. She turned and picked up her sandwich, running water into the pan to wash later.

"Wahine, did you do that? Run the water without touching the faucet?" Ky watched her take a bite of her sandwich.

Had she? She'd only just been thinking the dishes needed to soak. She chewed a few times searching for a connection to the water. Doing dishes sucked and she had wished they would do themselves.

"I guess I did. Cool. That's one more thing I didn't know I could do."

The men all stopped eating, some of them mid-chew.

Match set down his sandwich. "What else did you not know you could do?"

"A lot of things. But a few of the highlights were digging a hole up from Jakob's lair to his garden, tossing the snake guy into the air with the wind, and wrapping you all up in my plant protectors." She took another bite of her sandwich, letting those little nuggets sink in. They couldn't be any more surprised than she had been.

"Sweetheart, you didn't tell me you also had command of the water element." Jakob placed his hand on the back of her neck. He rubbed his thumb into her hair at the nape.

She looked around the table and wondered why the water was such a big deal. "I didn't know until now. I didn't know magic even existed until you brought me here, and Mrs. Bohacek told me I would burn your house down if I tried too hard to control my emotions around you."

"No." Match stood and shook his head. "Fire too?"

"And wind." Cage stood and placed his hands on the table.

"The water bent to her will. I had nothing to do with that." Ky nodded to her and stood with the other three.

Jakob moved to his feet and behind her, his front pressed to her back, giving her some comfort in this weird scenario.

"It can't be. There hasn't been one since the First Dragon's mate." Match looked her up and down with both a sense of awe and disbelief in his voice.

"You can't deny what we've seen." Ky said.

She looked from man to man. "What? What's going on?"

They didn't seem mad at her. But she'd obviously done something wrong. Maybe it had been a mistake to stay. She didn't know anything about this magical world she'd been dragged into. There were rules and a whole culture she knew nothing about.

At least with wedding planning and the world of her mother, she knew how to behave, how not to get on anyone's nerves.

Every move she made here made someone uncomfortable, including her.

Well, she was a woman and it was her prerogative to change her mind if she wanted to. That week off in Prague was sounding better all the time.

But she had told Jakob she'd stay.

Jakob turned her on her stool so that she faced him and had her back to the other men, probably to tell her he'd changed his mind. She wasn't what he thought she was, and it was time for her to go.

He searched her eyes, probably trying to find the best way to let her down. An empty place inside reopened, waiting to absorb the bad news. She couldn't let him see her disappointment. Never let them see you sweat. Or cry.

Ciara stared right back at him, doing her best to keep her face expressionless. The gas range behind him lit up like a bonfire. A breeze rattled the pots and pans hanging from the rack above their heads, and a misty fog and snowflakes filled the room, until there was only him and her.

Still Jakob didn't take his eyes off her. He did blink when a basil plant formed a crown around his head.

He raised a hand and ran his thumb over her lips then stroked his knuckles over her jaw. "I will never get enough of you. You, my curvy lover, are very special. How do you do it?"

Like she knew. She barely understood. "I thought they

were tied to emotions. Different emotions, different elements." That's how the woman in white had explained it.

Jakob shook his head and grinned at her. "Is that how you call on the power?"

Jakob's eyes flashed to her mouth and back up.

This was a confusing conversation. She had the distinct feeling they were only partly talking about magic. "You don't?"

The other men were mumbling in the background about not being able to see a thing. Good. She liked having Jakob to herself right now. The fog got thicker, and she heard someone bang into something and swear.

Jakob didn't notice, or if he did, didn't care. "No. I've used them to enhance it, like when the demon dragons attacked, I fueled a burst of power with anger. It's nothing like what you're doing now."

He moved even closer to her. So close she could taste the lust pouring off him. It was the flavor of cinnamon, just on the verge of being spicy.

"Okay." So he wasn't kicking her to the curb. That was good, right? She was so damn confused. If magic and mating were tied up in her own emotions, she was never going to get the hang of them.

"I don't understand why you think this is a big deal. You can do the same thing with the earth and plants and stuff."

"Zeleny, get your mate to drop the shield of fog. No one is going to harm her." Match's voice came through but muffled.

She wasn't ready to face the other guys yet. Jakob shook his head and rolled his eyes.

"Unless of course you've got your tongue down her throat or in other fun places, then by all means, keep the fog up." Cage piped in.

"Speak for yourself, Goldilocks. She's fucking fine and I wouldn't mind seeing her—" Ky's voice was cut off by an oomph.

Jakob continued on as if he was used to ignoring them. "Yes, one element. Every dragon can. Earth, fire, wind, and water. Four elements, four kinds of dragons. But none of us, nor any other being we know of commands more than one. Only one other witch in all time has wielded the same powers as you, commanding all four elements."

If this other witch was anything like Mrs. Bohacek, Ciara was sure she should meet her. "Who is she? Maybe I should talk to her. Get someone else to show me the ropes."

"She was the First Dragon's mate. And the mother of all Dragonkind. The White Witch."

Hmm. Could it be? Was the mysterious Mrs. Bohacek this White Witch? "You know that lady I told you about, the one who helped me escape the room and the lair?"

Jakob nodded, and she saw him putting the pieces together too.

"She taught me some of the basics of how to use the elements, by using them herself." There were some other vague memories of a discussion between Mrs. Bohacek and another man, but she couldn't quite grasp them now. "I think she might be your White Witch."

With a whoosh of hot wind, the fog around them disappeared.

"The White Witch and the First Dragon are gone. You couldn't have seen or talked to her." Match spat the words and when Ciara turned to look at him, smoke wafted up from his mouth and nostrils.

Cage flicked his wrist and blew the wisps of smoke away.

"There's something bigger going down here. We need to call an AllWyr."

Ky leaned forward. "I agree. We don't have enough info. All we know is that the relic's gone missing, the demon dragons are banding together to attack Jakob's lair in a horde, and now he's got a mate. We're missing something that's linking those all together."

"Jakob's witch is the key. She had the relic, and she has powers beyond what any witch should have, including an unexplainable hold on a Wyvern. How do we even know she's his true mate? She could be working a spell we've never seen before."

Jakob's soul shard shot light into the room like an explosion. The force of it literally knocked Match to the floor. He was back on his feet in an instant and charging at her. A red shimmer floated across his body and he shifted into a mean fire-breathing dragon, hell bent on eating Ciara.

WE BELONG TO EACH OTHER

*J*akob pushed Ciara behind him and down to the floor, before shifting into his dragon form. No one would question she was his mate or harm her.

His body filled the space, cracking the kitchen island and tossing it across the room. He thanked the First Dragon for his enormous size, because it also blocked Match. Jakob shoved the Red Wyvern out into the great room with a lash of his tail.

"Damn. I knew this would come to blows," Cage said.

Jakob trusted Cage and Ky to keep Ciara out of harm's way while he kicked the crap out of the red dragon who was supposed to be his mentor.

Match used his claws to dig into Jakob's shoulder, and tossed him so hard he broke through the window and wall landing in the garden. What the fuck was wrong with Match?

She's a charlatan, preying on your need for a mate.

He hadn't even known he needed a mate until he'd met her. He could have been perfectly happy dicking around for years until he was coerced into finding a companion to have an heir with.

Except he hadn't been with a woman in quite some time. Too damn long.

You have no idea what you're talking about, red. Jakob shook the debris off and barreled back into the house. He slammed into Match's side and plowed him through the living room, into the office, shattering the glass French doors, and landing them both in the garden.

I know more than you think, youngling. Match flipped them both and pinned Jakob to the ground.

That was a mistake. Jakob called upon the earth to open up, sucking them both underground. He turned and tunneled back to the surface and waited for Match's next move. Fire bellowed up through the tunnel he'd dug through the ground, burning the grass and shrubbery. Dick.

Ciara, Cage, and Ky ran out into the garden. Jakob snarled at the trio. *Get her out of here.*

"Don't you two touch me." She held up a hand and the two other Wyverns stayed where they were.

Dammit, he didn't want her to get hurt. *Ciara, sweetheart –*

"Don't sweetheart me, Jakob. I'm not going anywhere until this is resolved."

This is how dragons resolve their differences. Don't get in the middle of it. He didn't have a chance to warn her off any further because Match climbed out of the hole and jumped into the air.

Shit, he had to go and take this into the sky. Jakob unfurled his wings, but didn't get a chance to take off, because Match plopped to the ground, his wings frozen stiff.

Your witch did this to me.

Jakob glanced at Ciara and back to Match with his icicles

for wings squirming around on the ground. He shifted and burst into laughter.

"What's he laughing at?" Ciara asked the other Wyverns.

Cage and Kia joined in the chuckles. Ky pointed and added a layer of black ice underneath Match making him flail around even more. "It's pretty damn funny seeing a big bad fire dragon frozen like an ice lolly."

Shut up, you assholes and get her to melt this trap she's put on me.

"Melt your own damn ice." Jakob left Match to his freezer burn and walked straight over to Ciara, swooped her up into his arms and kissed her right there in front of everybody.

She blushed adorably, and the heat poured off of her. Cage and Ky both took a step back. Unfortunately, her warmth spread over to Match too and freed him from his icy bonds.

She'd shown him, shown them all her power. Hopefully that would satisfy Match.

The big red dragon shifted back into the dickhead.

"Do you need a further demonstration of her powers, or that my soul shard has chosen her for me?" Jakob wrapped an arm around her shoulders, pulling her to him as Match approached.

"Those could still be bewitching. There's only one way I will believe she's a true white witch or that you two belong together." Match folded his arms and glowered, a smug look on his face. "Give her the ring of Inanna."

Because Jakob was the Wyvern of the Green Dragons, his lair held many treasures besides gold, art, and heirloom seeds. Beneath their feet also rested the legacy of the dragon culture. The relic was only one part of the items under his protection.

"Who is Inanna and why do you want me to have her ring?"

Match had come up with the one test that would prove what Jakob already knew in his heart. Ciara was the one thing he never thought he'd have, what no dragon alive today thought they would see again in their lifetimes.

"If that's what it takes, then you will see she is my true mate."

"She'll have to find it first," Match growled.

"What do I have to find?" There was a hint of irritation in her tone.

"Inanna was the first and only white witch who had power of all the elements and the First Dragon's mate. She bequeathed a ring to the mate of every Wyvern as a test. A true mate could not only find the ring but was also gifted with power."

"And what happens if one is not a true mate?"

Jakob didn't know. His father had no mate, and his grandparents were gone long before then. He looked around to Cage and Ky, but they both shrugged. None of the three of them had even met their grandparents, much less been to a Wyvern mating ceremony. Which was why Jakob had never even sought to give Ciara the ring in the first place.

Match glared at Ciara. "The last ring in existence was my grandmother's. She fought a wicked battle against another witch who claimed to be my grandfather's true mate. When the other woman took the ring my grandmother found and put it on, the elements tore her apart."

Jakob waited for the knot of fear that statement had to form in his throat. But it didn't. Ciara would be fine, more than fine. She would rock the hell out of this challenge and put Match in his place once and for all.

But did she know that? Did she actually believe they were mates?

He would have to reassure her as they prepared for the ceremony.

Or maybe not. The wind whipped through her hair and that enticing fire lit up her eyes. She held out her hand, palm up, and motioned Match closer.

Match narrowed his eyes at her but deigned to lean down, eye to eye with her.

"Bring it on." Ciara turned on her heel and marched back into the house. The rest of them followed her while Match stayed outside smoking.

"Time to show us to your lair, you secretive bastard." Cage looked around the room as if he could spot the entrance.

Fuck. He was going to have to take them down there. But after losing the relic and the attack by the horde of demon dragons, he was going to have to move his treasure anyway.

"Not yet. This is not something to just pull out of our asses. Why don't you two go find out from the big red Dick in the garden how this ritual goes?"

"What are you two going to do?" Cage's tone implied exactly what he thought they were going to do.

"I'm going to help Ciara get ready."

"Yeah, I just bet you are." Ky winked at Ciara and waggled his eyebrows.

Jakob punched him in the arm and dragged Ciara away from the chance of any more innuendos from those two. He pulled her up the stairs and back to his room to do exactly what they had both implied.

He shut and locked the door behind them and watched as Ciara took in the veritable jungle of his bedroom. "I guess you like to have a lot of plants around, huh?"

He made the space as much like the outdoors as he possibly could. One side of the room was completely covered with a living wall. Moss and other small plants grew from floor to ceiling. He had a large king size bed, but spent most of his evenings sleeping in front of the fireplace on the mat of grass in a dragon-sized planter box.

He imagined taking her over and over in that grass, but today she would probably be more comfortable in a bed.

"What are we doing up here?"

"This." He picked her up in his arms and in three strides was across the room and dropping her into the bed. He didn't give her a chance to ask any more questions. He'd waited far too long and had three too many interruptions before getting her under him again. He crawled over her, caging her beneath his body and slid his tongue across her lips until she opened for him and returned the kiss.

Ciara reached down and grabbed the hem of his T-shirt and yanked it over his head. "I don't think this is what we are supposed to be doing."

"All of those supposed to's can go fuck themselves. I've been waiting to do this since we got back to the house." Match and the stick up his ass could wait a few more hours.

"I like how you think, dragon." She wrapped her thighs around his hips.

He loved how she was just as anxious to be with him as he was her.

"I want you to know that I don't need this test that Match has set up to prove you are my true mate." He brushed the hair away from her eyes and settled his hips against hers.

She wiggled under him almost making him forget what he'd wanted to say.

"You're not worried that I won't pass?" She bit her lip and he hated to see the bravado she'd displayed earlier fade from her eyes.

He captured that same lip between his teeth and sucked it into his mouth. He tasted and teased her tongue with his. He needed her and not just her body.

"Not even a little bit. Match doesn't understand, but even if he and the other Wyverns hadn't questioned whether you were my mate or not, they eventually would've seen how I've fallen for you."

She stilled. "You're not just saying that? It's not just this whole mating thing, is it?"

"Babe, you're everything I didn't even know I wanted in a mate. Your power, your fierceness, and the way you get a little crinkle between your eyes when you're coming. How could I not already be a little bit in love with you?"

"Love?"

"I know we started off bumpy, and we've only known each other for a short amount of time, but there's no other way to describe how I feel when I'm with you." He didn't let Ciara ask any more questions. If she was having a hard time believing the words, maybe she would understand the actions better.

He grabbed the edge of one of the rips in her dress and tore it more. He wrapped the strip of material around one of her wrists and secured it through a decorative notch on the headboard. He'd paid close attention to her responses when they'd been together before, and knew she got a sense of freedom out of this part of the submissive role.

The skin on her chest and neck flushed and she closed her eyes. "Did I say that I like how you think?"

"You didn't have to."

He tore more of her dress exposing the rest of her thighs to him. Later he'd be using those thighs as earmuffs. He loved the way she smelled and tasted.

"Wait, what if I want you to, well what I mean to say is…"

"What, cupcake? Tell me what you want, what you like."

"How do you feel about doggy style?"

He sliced the knot he'd already tied open and flipped Ciara onto her stomach. "You mean dragon style."

He ground against her pushing the hard ridge of his cock still covered by his pants against the cleft of her ass.

"Oh God, yes I did."

He was about out of material so instead he grew the small tree near the bed so that a branch looped around the bottom of the headboard. "Grab onto that and don't let go until I tell you to."

He waited until she had her fists wrapped tightly around the wood before he lifted her ass into the air. The remaining fabric bunched and fell away so that her soft white skin was fair for him to touch. Or spank.

"Oh," she cried out when he slapped her ass the first time.

"Do you like that, Ciara?" Pink spread across one of her ass cheeks. Please say yes, please say yes.

"Yes. But I'd like it even better if you did it while you were fucking me."

Dirty, dirty fucking witch.

Jakob yanked down his pants without even unbuttoning or unzipping, shredding them and tossing them aside. His cock pointed the way, knowing exactly where he wanted to be. He slipped two fingers inside of her, making sure she was ready for him. She pushed her ass back, grinding onto his fingers. She wasn't just wet for him, she was soaking. He didn't wait another second before sliding into her.

"Ooh, you feel even bigger inside of me from this position."

He smacked her ass and watched the little pucker of her hole tighten. So damn sexy. He sunk into her wet heat over and over, reveling in her gasps and moans. Each and every one of them was his. Each time he spanked her she would groan and clench both her pussy and her ass. He used his other thumb to circle and tease her pucker. "Tell me you'd like to have me here too."

She shuddered, and he felt the contractions of her inner muscles clench around him.

"Yes, yes I would."

That was all he needed to hear. With his cock still buried deep in her cunt, he gently pushed the tip of his thumb in to her asshole. Then he slapped her ass again and she cried out his name.

"Jakob, that's going to make me come."

"That orgasm is mine, don't you dare take it until I tell you to."

That husky whimper he loved to hear came from deep in her throat. He increased his rhythm sliding his cock in and out of her, spanking her over and over.

"Please," she sucked in great lungful of air, "please, Jakob I need to come."

He was going to make her come so hard she saw stars. He waited until he felt her pussy fluttering around his cock and then moved his thumb, matching the rhythm in and out of her sensitive tissue.

"That's it my love. Let me hear you scream. Come for me, Ciara." She sank her face into the pillows and the branch in her hands broke in half before her body buckled under him. The force of the contractions squeezed him so hard and tight that her orgasm became his. If every time they had sex it got better, pretty soon they would never leave the bedroom.

Ciara crumpled underneath of him and he lay down beside her wrapping her in the blankets and his arms, and cocooning them in his wings. What could he say but she brought the beast out in him.

He'd never lost control of his dragon shift, except around her.

She was asleep instantly. He grinned, loving the fact that he'd fucked her to sleep.

It had been a long few days for them both. But while she rested, he had work to do. As soon as she seemed settled, he slipped out of bed and into the en suite bathroom. He cleaned himself and grabbed clean washcloths to use on her.

She moaned a little when he wiped the warm cloth across her body but didn't wake up.

Jakob watched her sleep and sent up another prayer to the First Dragon.

He threw on some clothes and crept out and all the way down to his lair.

Inanna's ring was exactly where it should be in a smaller cave off the side of the larger cavern, where he stored all of the items important to dragon lore. He would leave it where it was, for Ciara to find later. He opened a chest next to the stand the ring was on and rooted through until he found what he was looking for. He hoped she would like it.

He slipped back into the room, hoping she would still be asleep and that they might have time for one more round before Match and the other Wyverns got tired of waiting.

Jakob slid a box on the bed. It was one of those large rectangular boxes he'd seen in the movies with feathery tissue paper and a gorgeous gown inside. He'd love to see her twirl around holding it to her chest.

Ciara rolled over and blinked sleepy eyes at him. "Where did you go?"

"To get you this."

He'd never given a woman a gift like this before. God, he hoped he'd done a good job and that she liked it. Women were weird about gifts and especially clothing. It wasn't like she could go return it and get a handbag or something instead.

"Open it."

"Come back to bed."

"Open the box, my love."

She glanced at it and tried to hide her smile. "Fine, but only because I'm insanely curious about what's inside." She lifted the lid and slid open the layers of tissue paper. "Oh, Jake, it's so beautiful."

A dress with hues of teal, jade, and gold, like a tropical island oasis made of silk and fairy dust sparkled in the box. "I can't wear it."

"Why not?"

"It breaks every fashion rule don't for the plus-size girl. I'll look like giant couch masquerading as a bright green disco ball and it's pretty impractical for a treasure hunt, don't you think?"

"Those sound like stupid rules. You'll look beautiful and this is a special occasion."

"Nobody has ever bought me a dress before besides my mother."

"Put it on." When this mess was over he'd buy her a new dress every week just so he could see how her face lit up at the gifts. Besides, it gave him the perfect excuse to undress her. Like he was going to do right now.

She pushed the box away and shook her head. "No."

He slid the tattered sleeve of the top of the dress she still wore down her arm and followed his hand with kisses. "Yes."

She gasped softly. "Don't think that because I let you get

bossy with me in the bedroom that you can tell me what to do anytime or anywhere else."

"We are in the bedroom, cupcake."

She laughed and wagged her finger at him. "And we won't get out of it if you don't stop that."

"I'm not sure I have a problem with that." In fact, he didn't. Once this damn ritual was over and Ciara was officially his mate in the eyes of the AllWyr, he'd spend hours, days, a month at least making love to her.

"Naughty dragon. I have to go prove to your friends that we belong together."

Her words alone were nothing to make him worry. He knew they were meant for each other. The slight wobble in her voice made him want to kill someone.

He traced his fingers over her dragon mark. "I'll tell them to fuck off if you want me to."

"No." She took his hand in hers. "We have enough other problems what with that horde of snake people. I have a horrible feeling we haven't seen the end of them, have we?"

He'd almost forgotten about the demon dragons and the missing relic. "Afraid not."

Ciara slid out from under the covers, taking the sheet with her and wrapping it around her body. She climbed out of the bed looking like a goddess. "I didn't think so. But we can fight them off together."

The thought of having Ciara fight by his side both terrified him and turned him on. The sex afterwards would be incredible.

"Come on. Let's get ready for the ring ritual and get the rest of the Wyverns the hell out of here. Because I'm looking forward to fucking you in every single room of this villa."

The glimmer in her eye and the naughty grin on her face

told him she liked that idea. "How many rooms does this place have?"

"Nine bedrooms, two great rooms, a kitchen, an office, and don't forget about the lair. I'm pretty sure I have some golden handcuffs hiding down there somewhere."

THE TRIAL AND THE RING

*J*akob brought Ciara and the rest of the Wyverns down to his lair. He grumped and growled the entire way and this time they took the stairs instead of jumping over the edge. She was half disappointed about that.

The five of them stood just inside the doorway, staring into the vast space. How was she supposed to find one little ring in all this stuff?

Jakob held her hand tightly in his. He looked so damn handsome in the fancy suit he put on. All of the guys had donned dress clothes too. A few more dragon shifters, if they were all this good looking, and she'd have herself a calendar.

She fiddled with the material on her dress and wondered if this was similar to the nerves her brides felt. She'd seen more than one of them practically rub a hole through satin and charmeuse fidgeting.

"You'll do fine, love." He pulled her fingers away from the dress and kissed each of the fingertips.

"I know." She believed that he believed she was his true

mate and had the ability to turn on some sort of internal GPS device. So, she would pretend she believed it too.

"If you two are done making eyes at each other, shall we begin?" Match was as grumpy as ever, even if he did look like a Mr. December candidate in his Armani suit and red silk tie.

Jakob didn't reply and looked to her for confirmation. He might be bossy and dominant in the bedroom, which she loved, but this gentlemanly side of him the rest of the time was very endearing. He didn't assume, he didn't demand, and he didn't make her feel like she had to always try harder and be nicer just for a little of his attention.

There was no one else in her life like that. Too bad it had taken being kidnapped by a dragon to realize it.

"Let's get this reality show on the road." The last few days of her life would make riveting TV, that no one would believe for a second was real. She hardly did herself. Now she was at the point where she either accepted and won the challenge or got kicked off the island. She was pretty sure if they did an anonymous ballot, Match would be the one everyone voted to get rid of. He was such a drama llama.

All eyes were now on her. She took a deep breath hoping for some magical beam of light, or sixth sense would guide her way. The ring could be anywhere, and it would take her a thousand years and then some to search through every chest, shelf, box, and pile of treasure to find this one tiny item.

Might as well start with an area she was familiar with. She crawled over the same pile of coins she had the last time she was here. Up ahead just to the right, was the towering shelves of paintings she'd almost burned to the ground. Except only the wood seemed a little singed now and all of the artwork was intact. She made her way around the shelf and found that same table and chairs set up like a little café in a cave.

This time, though, instead of a teapot and a tiered tray of treats, in the middle of the table sat a small carved wooden box. It was the perfect size to hold a ring. Ciara sat down at the table, not sure she could remain standing. What if this was it?

Could it have possibly been this easy?

She hadn't even used any of her newfound powers or gotten a sign from above, or anything. She slid the box in front of her and popped open the lid. Inside on a bed of Moss was a tarnished and worn gold ring. It resembled something one might get when they graduated from high school or an Academy. The top was circular and divided into four quadrants, each with a small but brilliant jewel inlaid into the gold. In the center sat a brilliant diamond that sent sparkles of light out into the darkness.

Her memory flashed to the necklace she'd been wearing when Jakob found her. The same one that had disintegrated into a handful of dusty dragon scales.

She heard a voice from someone nearby and hid in the hallway adjacent to the kitchen. But she didn't want to hide. She wanted to ask whoever belong to that voice where she was, and when he'd touched it. The design was identical.

Ciara sat at the table for another moment staring at the beautiful piece of jewelry. Match had said Inanna, the mate of the First Dragon, had given it to his grandmother when she had fallen in love with his grandfather.

Her mind whirled and swirled. Someone had given her that necklace and she knew the same as two plus two that it was the same person who'd left the ring on the table for her. Ciara closed the lid of the box and carried it back to the entrance of the lair.

"Giving up so soon, little witch? Well, that's probably for

the best." Match and Jakob both stared at her as she climbed over the pile of gold and stepped up in front of them.

Where Match's face was filled with derision, Jakob's was concerned.

"Everything okay?"

She winked at Jakob and slapped the ring box into Match's hand. Match gently opened the lid and stared silently at the ring inside it. Cage and Ky came over and peered down into his hand.

Ciara turned her back on them all and walked into Jakob's arms. "I found it."

"You didn't even have time to get all the way to the side cave where I keep all of the dragon heirlooms."

"You knew where it was?" She couldn't have expected him to tell her, but she was a little surprised. "Doesn't matter, I didn't go into any kind of cave. It was on a table near your rack of paintings."

"Ciara, I know every single thing that is in this cavern, down to the tiniest jewel and each individual coin. There is no table here."

"Somehow, that doesn't surprise me. It looks more like it came from a garage sale than anywhere else. I think I know who put it there." She paused, considering whether she should tell him her theory or not. She knew so little about their lore, but what pieces she knew all fit together. "I'm afraid your lair is haunted, because Inanna is or was here."

"She left the ring for you, didn't she?" Jakob said the words with reverence.

Ciara nodded but didn't get a chance to tell him anything else. Match marched over and interrupted their conversation. "Put it on."

He shoved the ring box back to her, but Jakob intercepted it.

"She'll wear this ring," his voice filled the cavern, "when you read the ritual, and I put it on her finger."

Match's left eye twitched, but he nodded.

Jakob had retrieved a very old looking book from a nearby shelf and handed it over to Match. He nodded to Cage and Ky, who took up on either side of her and Jakob. Match flipped the book open and began reciting words that sounded vaguely Middle Eastern to her. She didn't understand any of them except when he said her name and then Jakob's. Jakob responded in the same language as if he had been asked a question and said her name.

Then both Jakob and Match looked at her like she had something to say. Match rolled his eyes. Jakob grabbed her hands and said, "repeat after me."

She nodded and listened to the foreign syllables so that she could say them back to him.

"*Ni*, Ciara Mosley-Willingham *cad men anna ni gud* Jakob Zeleny." The cadence of the sentence felt oddly familiar. She'd heard something similar to it before, but she couldn't quite put her finger on when or where. It wasn't like she spoke any foreign languages.

She repeated as much as she could back to him. "*Ni*, Ciara Mosley-Willingham, *cad…*"

"*cad men anna ni gud –*" Jakob prompted her.

"*cad men anna ni gud* Jakob Zeleny." As she finished the sentence, Jakob took her hand and slid the ring on her finger.

Ciara had to blink fast to hold back the tears forming on her eyelashes. They had just bubbled up out of nowhere. Seeing Jakob put the ring on her finger made her think of all of the times she'd seen a groom slide a wedding band on to a bride's hand.

She'd love to experience the real deal for herself. She didn't even know if dragons had weddings.

She planned her own in her head a million times. The flowers, the venue, the cake, and even the groom changed over the years. But what always remained the same was knowing she'd finally found the right one.

Not someone who completed her, because she was her own woman, but a man who loved her and wanted her, who'd chosen her above all others. A man whom she'd chosen too.

She might not ever have that, if Jakob was right and destiny had taken that choice from them both and put them together. The feeling inside of her chest was the same, like a warm glow. Like that feeling she'd had on a snowy day in her childhood when she was chilled to the bone and then climbed into bed with an electric blanket. A shiver rolled across her skin in the exact same way, waking up all of her nerve endings and telling them everything would be all right.

Jakob grabbed her up in his arms and kissed her. His tongue pressed at her lips asking for entrance, and she opened for him. For a moment she forgot anyone else was around and lost herself in Jakob's kiss.

Match read something more from the book then closed it shut with a pop. Jakob gave her one more taste and then pulled away. The smile on his face was so big that she couldn't help but return it. Ky slapped her on the back and Cage shook Jakob's hand.

His smile was the last thing she saw before the world around her went black and she fell into a whirlwind of light and sound and colors that made her nauseated.

When the world stopped spinning, Ciara no longer saw

the cavern around her. She was in some sort of apartment kitchen. There was a refrigerator, a sink, a microwave, a small table and chairs, and plants on every available surface and hanging from the ceiling. They looked like herbs, yes that was a basil plant, and she was pretty sure that was cilantro on the windowsill.

She wanted to reach out and touch the leaves, but her hands and arms were not responding. She blinked and glanced all around the room, not sure what she was looking for. Then she reached into pocket on her long white flowing gown and pulled out a necklace. When had she put on this dress? What happened to the beautiful one that Jakob had given her?

She laid the necklace on the table and saw two things where there should only be one.

At the bottom of the chain was a pendant with a tree and a serpent. But it was also a colorful collection of scales.

A muffled voice came from somewhere nearby, and Ciara quickly hid in the hallway. But wait. She didn't want to hide. She wanted to find anyone she could talk to, ask how she had gotten here, and where here was.

She couldn't move. She had no control over her own body, like she was possessed.

A key turned in a lock and door opened. The voice she'd heard became louder and clearer.

"No, mom, stay there. You will be more comfortable spending the summer as a flower. I'll be fine here."

The voice was speaking English with an American accent. Not only was she not in the cavern anymore, she wasn't even in the Czech Republic, she wasn't even in Europe.

A pretty young woman came into the kitchen talking on a

cell phone. She dropped a bag of groceries on the counter and opened the nearest cupboard door.

Ciara tried everything to force her body to do her bidding. Even if she could call out to the woman, that would at least be something.

The woman held the cell phone between her ear and her shoulder while she pulled a set of martini glasses out and set them in the sink. "Yeah, the kids at school are really taking to the garden. I'm doing my best to help their little green thumbs along."

She ran water in the sink and Ciara missed a few words of the conversation. Not that it seemed that important. She was just some girl talking to her mom on the phone.

The woman pulled one of the glasses out, but it slipped in her wet hands and fell towards the floor. She didn't even flinch. One of the leaves on the basil plant on the counter next to her quadrupled in size, swooped down, and caught the glass before it hit the floor.

Whoa. The only other time she had seen plants do anything like that was when either she or Jakob asked them for help. The plants in this kitchen were doing the same for the woman on the phone.

So, was she a witch or a dragon?

No, Jakob had said there was no such thing as female dragons. A witch then.

Oh my God. Jakob had thought that Ciara had stolen the First Dragon's relic and had been working with a coven of witches to do it. Could this woman be involved in the theft of the relic?

She had something on her kitchen table that belonged in Jakob's lair, if it belonged anywhere.

Ciara needed to get her hands on it.

"Yes, the party is this weekend. I'll be fine. It's not like anything could happen to me with so many shifters around."

Shifters? Yeah, this woman was more than a schoolteacher.

She said some goodbyes and hung up the phone, then set it on the table. That's when she saw the necklace.

Damn. Ciara had been hoping she wouldn't find it.

"That's not like her." The woman picked up the necklace and twirled it in her hand. "It is pretty."

She opened the clasp and put the necklace on. The leaves on the tree, and the eye of the serpent glowed with the same green light as Jakob's shard.

There was something very strange going on here.

A warm white light surrounded Ciara and the world spun again.

This time Ciara couldn't figure out where she was. There was nothing around her. Like nothing. No sky, no ground, no horizon.

"You were sure the little flower has to be next? I think it's too soon."

She recognized that voice. It was the man who had been with Mrs. Bohacek in the cavern.

Suddenly, his face was in front of her, and her hand was on his cheek. "Yes, love. It's time. She's been waiting for too long."

The man took her hand and kissed her palm. "And I'd have her wait another five thousand years, if it would keep her safe."

"We can't keep her safe forever."

The man growled, and colorful scales shimmered across his body.

"Come now, everything will be all right. Let's go where we can watch this one unfold."

"The Galla dragons are already gathering. He'd better fucking claim her soon."

Jakob had already claimed her, who is this man talking about?

"Yes, dear. But he has to meet her first."

Ciara snapped her fingers and the white light disappeared. The world fell out from beneath her and she tumbled into an abyss.

This time she was sure she was going to throw up. She scrunched her eyes tight and swallowed, trying to keep the bile down.

"Ciara. Ciara, can you hear me? Ciara" Jakob's voice was frantic, and she could feel his hands running over her body.

She opened her eyes and jolted from the lack of movement. She wasn't falling, she was laying on the floor of the cavern.

Dark faces were staring down at her. She blinked and tried to focus. The first one she recognized was Cage. He shook his head like she'd just performed a death defying circus act. "I seriously can't believe you aren't dead."

While she appreciated the sentiment, his was not the one she cared about.

Ky grinned at her. "Sweet as."

Where was Jakob? She needed to tell him what had happened.

"Thank the First Dragon. Are you okay?" Jakob propped her up with one arm and held her cheek in the other, turning her head so he could examine her face.

"I think I know where the First Dragon's relic is." Her voice was her own again. She wiggled her fingers to make sure she could. Her body responded to her this time. She felt normal again.

"The relic?" Jakob asked.

"Where?" Ciara glanced up at Match, who looked like he'd aged ten years. "What did you see?"

"I don't really understand, but I think I was with, or in, sharing a body with someone. She gave the First Dragon's relic to another witch. One who commands plants."

"An earth witch. Where is she?"

"I can't be sure. All I saw was the inside of an apartment. But I'm pretty sure it was in America."

"That's my girl."

Uh, that's not what she expected him to say.

Jakob helped her to her feet and she leaned on him, still feeling woozy. "Let's get you upstairs and into bed. I need to hold you in my arms for a damned long time."

That sounded nice.

"Not going to have your wedding night?"

Wedding?

Wedding night?

"What is that supposed to mean?" Ciara pulled out of Jakob's arms and turned to look at him.

Cage took a step back. "You didn't tell her?"

If someone didn't explain to her exactly what was going on, she was going to call up one hell of a tempest and whip them all up into a tornado. "Tell me what? What's going on?"

Ky tried to interject. "That ceremony—"

Jakob lashed out and arm. "Shut. Up."

Ky raised his hands, giving up.

Jakob took her hand in his and played with the ring on her finger. "The ritual is an important one to dragons. One that hasn't been performed by anyone for a long time. It was, I guess is again, a part of the mating process for Wyverns."

"And?" She was pretty damn sure she already knew where

this was going. Just how long was it going to take Jakob to wind his way to the truth?

"When a Wyvern is mated, the other three Wyverns must acknowledge the mate."

"You mean they have to approve of me." She knew Match never would be happy about her being in Jakob's life.

"No, they must recognize the union. A Wyvern may consult his mate on Wyr decisions. They need to understand we are a single unit. But you're my mate no matter what."

She could think of some whats that didn't matter at the moment.

"They do that by standing up and witnessing that ritual."

That and the words they'd said were the part that worried her the most. "What were the words you had me repeat. The *ni man can anna* stuff?"

"*Ni cad men anna ni gud.*" He said the words again, slowly

"Yeah. That. What does that mean?"

"I bind myself to you, warrior."

He'd said the same to her. Wedding vows.

Then he'd put a ring on her finger and kissed her.

They'd just been married. No planning, no getting to taste a thousand cakes, no inviting family and friends to witness the blessed occasion, and no fucking flowers.

She was going to kill him.

CAN'T DO IT

J akob envisioned carrying Ciara up the stairs, curling their bodies together for hours, until the other Wyverns were ready to go on the hunt for the relic. He needed to take care of her.

That's not what was currently happening.

His lady love had stormed out of the lair, and when he said stormed, he meant hundred mile an hour winds, thunder and lightning, and hail that fucking stung as it pelted him and the other Wyverns in the face.

Match was oddly sulking instead of blowing his top with his fiery temper. His flames could have dried them all in an instant, but Ky was the only one who was still dry since he'd been smart enough to command the water away from himself.

Cage plucked chunks of ice out of his hair. "Man, you should have told her what the ritual meant before we all got dressed up."

"There wasn't time." He'd always choose making love to her over explaining out-of-date rituals that no one had used in almost a century. Who fucking cared about the silly words and ceremony?

Apparently, she did.

First, he'd take care of the Wyr business and then he'd go find his mate and figure out exactly what was wrong and how much groveling he needed to do to fix it.

"Ky, you think you can use that nose of yours to find the relic with what Ciara told you?"

Ky stroked his chin. "I'd like a little more to go on than 'America'. That country is fucking huge. I can't scent the relic either. Haven't been able to since before we got here. Something more powerful than your angry mate is using some fancy-ass magic to hide it."

"We should all go." Match stood off to the side, away from the rest of the group. He hadn't said anything for several minutes, which was completely unlike him. "A massive demon dragon attack on a Wyvern, a white witch mate, and the relic being used by an unknown entity aren't signs we can ignore. Something big is happening and we'd better figure out what."

"You are acknowledging that Ciara is my mate." Jakob didn't make it a question. If a temper tantrum rain storm was all it took to get Match's head out of his ass, he wished he'd pissed Ciara off earlier. She had proven herself as a true mate and had hardly blinked twice about the trial.

There was no way Match could object any more. She was powerful, she was beautiful, she was smart, and Jakob loved her.

Yes. By the First Dragon, he absolutely loved her.

The feelings in his heart stretched and grew like a seed pushing up through the soil for the first time. It had been dark for so long, dormant because of his belief that he would never have a mate. This new sensation felt incredible.

This wasn't just a result of the mating or the ritual that compelled him to be with her, to protect her. It controlled his lust for her.

Even if none of those factors pushed him toward her, he still would have fallen head over tail for her. He didn't want to spend any more time with these yahoos.

He'd give them five more minutes of his attention and then he was blasting his way out of here to go find Ciara.

Match cleared his throat and Jakob half expected smoke rings to come out of his mouth. Flashes of some emotion he'd never seen on Match flashed through his eyes. Regret?

Instead he got an apology.

"I, above all, never expected any of us to have mates, and only wanted to protect the Wyrs. I still can't believe it, but she has proven herself. I apologize to you and your mate for the… distress."

Match had pushed, but Jakob hadn't done enough to stand up for Ciara, to protect her. It never should have come to this.

Match clasped his hand on Jakob's shoulder, and he returned the gesture. "Take care of her well, brother warrior. You have been blessed like no other among us probably ever will be."

"I will." Oh, how he would.

"Good. We'll make the preparations to travel to America. You see to the care and feeding of your mate."

One more thing. A prescient fate must have been in his office with him two days ago, because he'd gotten the ball rolling on this investigation in the right direction.

"I sent Steele there to see if he could find out anything about who had taken the relic in the first place. Contact your red, Daxton, to see if they've made any progress. We can start with whatever they've found."

Match and the others nodded, and Jakob, as much as it pained him, took his leave. He shifted into his dragon form to exit the lair as fast as possible. He had an angry mate to tend to. Which he planned to do with a lot of kissing and other darker pleasures.

He followed her scent up to his bedroom where he found her still storming, pacing back and forth and muttering to herself.

Ciara, come to me.

She stopped mid-stride and pointed a shaking finger at him. If he didn't know better, he'd think she was cursing him.

"I am not talking to you like that. You turn back into a man right now, so I can look you in the eye, mister."

She'd banked her powers for now, no tornadoes or dust devil accompanied her demand, however, her face was flushed and her body was tense.

He'd help her work all that tension out. He shifted, ready to let the words of love pour out of his mouth and into her heart.

"I can't believe you robbed me of planning my own wedding. Do you know how long I've been dreaming of this day?" She threw up her hands and returned to her angry stomp stomp stomp across the room, to the window and back.

Ah. So that was it. He could explain and then they could get to the love declarations and kissing. "I did not rob you of anything, my little thief."

She folded her arms around herself. "Did we, or did we not just star in a ceremony where I wore a special gown, you wore a special suit?"

What did that have to do with anything? He thought she'd

like the dress and he wanted to look his best for her. "Yes. We did. But—"

"And did friends and family witness an exchange of vows that binds us together for as long as we both shall live?"

Not that they'd needed the ceremony, its ritual, or any words to bind them together. They were mated. They'd be together forever. In this world and the next.

"Yes. You and me for the next four-hundred and fifty years or so."

That was also news he probably shouldn't just spring on her. Her lifespan would now match his. Her aging would slow and she would remain her luscious twenty-something self for as long as he was still in his Prime. A big adjustment for a human.

If she heard him, she either didn't care or wasn't ready to discuss it, because she continued her tirade. If she would just let him explain that the ritual wasn't important, that they were bound together the second they first met. Then they could commence with the love making portion of the evening.

"And if we didn't have to go running off to America to find the relic, would we now be expected to entertain those guests with food and drinks, music and dancing?"

She was completely fixated on this. Could she really be this upset about a dumb ceremony or was there something else bothering her and this was the convenient fight to pick?

"I guess so." He wasn't exactly sure on the protocol for after a Wyvern mating ritual, but a party felt in order.

"Was there supposed to be a cake?" Her voice was getting shriller with each question.

Maybe she wanted the party. "If you want one."

"That, my dear mate," she spat the word at him, "is the very definition of a wedding."

Jakob crossed the room and stood in front of her so close she had to tilt her head up to look at him. The fire, ice, wind, and lush green in those eyes took his breath away. He didn't want to fight with her. He wanted to make love to her. "Ciara. Calm down."

That was apparently the wrong thing to say, because every plant in the room wilted, the petals fell off the blooms, and one small pot he'd been preparing to put seedlings in burst into flames.

"Don't tell me how to feel." Her voice was quiet, but the wind whipping through the room at gale force wasn't. "You're the one who brought up all these, these...feelings in me, dammit. So, don't go expecting me to shove them back inside. I won't and I'm going to have to learn how to deal with that."

Emotional women were not exactly his forte. He couldn't remember the last time someone had yelled at him. People didn't raise their voices to Wyverns. He had said he wanted to see her riled because she was gorgeous lit up this way. He ought to be more careful what he wished for, because he wouldn't be surprised if she, of all women, sudden learned how to breathe fire.

"Ciara, sweetheart –"

"Don't you sweetheart me, Jakob Zeleny. Do you have any idea what my entire life has been about for the past eight years?"

He did know how to answer that question because the answer was 'not a fucking clue'. But that probably wasn't what she wanted him to say. At this point no matter what he said he would probably be wrong. He wasn't even a hundred percent sure whether she was mad about not understanding the words to the mating ceremony or that it had all happened without her say so on the flowers and decorations.

She had asked him a question about her life back in America, so maybe she was upset that she would be leaving that behind.

That was something they definitely hadn't discussed. Okay, he could see how she would be mad about that. Good. He would dig in and get to know every part of her psyche, so she wouldn't have to be sad or mad anymore. He wanted his mate to be happy.

Happy mate, happy fate.

"I don't, but if you'll just tell me what you're really upset about, I will do my best to fix it for you."

He patted himself on the back for that. He might be new to being a mate, but he knew that they took care of each other. If she needed to have a job to feel comfortable and happy, he'd buy her whatever company she wanted.

"I'm trying to tell you why I'm mad. I'm a wedding planner, asshat."

Uh-oh. They were back to the creative name calling. "I'm sure there are plenty of couples in the Czech Republic who need help planning their own weddings. That's not really a dragon thing, but once I call the household staff back, some of the women can probably help point you in the right direction."

"No, jackass. It's not about other people's weddings. I wanted to be able to plan my own. Now it's too damn late." She held up her ring finger in a gesture that almost looked obscene.

That wasn't what bothered Jakob. It was the tears gathering in her eyes. She turned her back on him before any of them fell. It didn't matter because his gut told him, with the empty burn spreading from the pit of his stomach to his throat, that he was too late to stop them.

He hadn't spent an entire minute in his whole life thinking about a wedding. He certainly never thought he'd have one, even if he did find a mate. He didn't consider the ritual they had just performed a wedding.

He reached out and touched her shoulder, planning to pull her into his arms and comfort them both. She jerked away and walked to the other side of the room.

What did she want from him, want him to say or do to make this better? Aha. "We can have a human wedding if you want to. Invite a thousand people. There are churches dotted all over this country or we could have it in the back garden."

She shook her head and rubbed her forehead. Suddenly the fire was burnt out in her. "I don't think so. This," she waved her hand back and forth between them, "isn't going to work."

Wait a minute. What was she talking about?

"Ciara." He closed the gap between them in an instant and pulled her into his arms whether she wanted to be there or not. He needed to feel her there.

She placed her hands flat against his chest. "We don't even know each other. You know nothing about me, and I barely even understand what you are, much less who. Your world is filled with magic and demons and dragons. All things I had no idea existed outside of fairytales until a couple of days ago."

They had time to get to know each other. Hundreds of years. As soon as this business with the relic was taken care of he'd devote a thousand percent of his attention to her. Until then, she simply needed to know she belonged. Not only to him, but in the world of the dragon warriors. Mates were revered, and she being the first of this generation, even more so. "You're a part of that world now. You've got more magic in your little toes then most witches have in their entire body."

"Maybe, but I've lived twenty-eight years without it, it'll be easy enough to go back to that."

"And what about the dragons?" It was one dragon in particular he was asking about. Could she go back to living without him?

"I can't live with...can't be in love with someone I hardly know."

He was.

"We'll get to know each other then. What's your favorite ice cream flavor?" He knew more than enough to know he was in love with her. She could ask him anything and he'd answer honestly.

"It doesn't really matter. I want to go home Jakob. Back to my life, my job, my friends, and forget all of this ever happened."

No.

He'd only just found her. She couldn't leave, forget about him. They were soul mates.

Jakob's soul shard glowed, and Ciara looked away.

Why did that hurt so bad?

She already had his soul, maybe he should give her the shard containing a small piece of it to her.

No one he'd ever known had done such a thing. The soul shard was every dragon's most prized possession. A piece of the First Dragon's soul intertwined with a part of their own. He and every dragon received it at the age of forty, roughly equivalent to seven in human years.

He'd never taken it off in the hundred and twenty or so years since then.

As a little boy he'd felt like the biggest badass in the world the first time he'd shifted after receiving his soul shard. What would happen if he did give it to Ciara?

She didn't have any dragon blood in her, so he doubted she'd shift. Her powers continued to amaze him though.

Would giving it to her be enough to prove he believed they belonged together, not separated by an ocean?

He could only try.

But what if she truly didn't want it? She was right that this wasn't her world. Hadn't been. The significance of the gesture may be lost on her.

He fingered the talisman, feeling its warmth in his hand. He would wait. Just until she decided to stay, to keep the commitment she'd made.

"Ciara. I don't want you to go. You mean everything to me now. I am sorry you feel cheated out of your wedding plans, and I will make it up to you any way that I can. Stay, my love."

"Please, don't call me that. We aren't in love. Lust maybe, more likely it's something to do with the crazy and scary events of the past few days. It's the adrenaline talking. Couples who fall in love during dangerous situations rarely last."

All the warmth and magic had faded from Ciara's voice. She sounded like a robot repeating lines it had been programmed to say. She'd been adamant about letting all her feelings out. She was burying them instead.

She was less emotional now than when he'd first kidnapped her.

Her emotions were completely quashed. Burning down the house.

How could he reach her now? She'd been the most alive, the most free when he'd dominated her. If he didn't give her a chance to think and analyze she might let go of this ridiculous notion that they didn't belong together.

Jakob slid his hands down her arms, lightly skimming across her skin and took her wrists in each of his hands. He needed to do this next part carefully.

He raised her arms. She resisted at first, but then allowed him to push them up and over her head, then back to wrap around his neck.

The position thrust her chest out pushed her ass back into him, her soft plump rear caressing his cock through his trousers.

"You're mine, Ciara," he whispered in her ear and nibbled on the shell of her ear.

She shivered, her moans so quiet he wasn't sure he'd heard her. "Don't."

"Ask me to stop and I will. Don't ask me to, and I'll prove to you just how much you belong to me."

She didn't move, except to tilt her head to the side, baring the mark. Yes.

His lips found the tattoo, then his tongue, and his teeth. He bit down hard, reclaiming her and making sure she knew it. She sucked in a gasp and wilted in his arms.

This wasn't submission, she was entranced again.

Fuck, shit, fucking shit.

He lifted her and carried her to the bed, ready to call out to the others. But her body tensed, shook, and then she opened her eyes.

"Kur-jara is coming. We must stop him before he finds her."

The voice coming from her mouth was not her own. The dragon mark on her neck writhed as if trying to escape her skin, to rise up and protect her.

His own dragon tattoo stretched its wings, reaching for her. How could he protect her if he could feel, see, or find the enemy? Who the hell was Kur-jara and was the woman he searched for Ciara or another?

"Ciara, can you hear me? Wake up."

She shivered and her body went limp.

"Ciara, come back to me."

Her breathing returned to normal and her eyelids fluttered. She struggled to open them and when she did, they were unfocused.

"Jakob?"

"I'm here. What did you see? Are you okay?"

"Go to America. Quickly. Find the flower." Her words were slurred.

Jakob didn't think she even knew what she was saying. "I'm not leaving you."

The other Wyverns could go to America. He was not moving from Ciara's side ever again.

AMERICA OR BUST

iara's mind swirled in a black ocean. No. Wherever she was, it wasn't wet, but soft and smelled of dirt. She'd been there a long time. But it was okay. She had her mate.

But where were her children?

She woke with a start. Under her was a soft bed, Jakob's body wrapped around hers, his wings unfurled and lay on top of them like an emerald green cocoon.

What had she been dreaming about? A dark presence, something that scared her, and children. Her children.

She shook her head. She didn't have children and probably never would.

Dread overwhelmed her, pricking at her heart, making it skip beats to keep up with the pace the adrenaline required of her body.

Something very dark was coming. No, it wasn't coming here. It was in America. Home.

She needed to go home. Not that she had anyone or anything to go home to. Yes, her job had been important to her, it had been her life. The one thing that had made her mother, not exactly proud of her, more like tolerating of her.

And Wes? How could she have ever thought her crush on him was anything like love?

Funny how a few days with Jakob had changed everything. She would never get over him. But she could not see any way their relationship would work out in the long term.

He'd needed her to find the relic, and she'd needed him to fill a whole host of unmet needs. That's all this was. One hell of a whirlwind fling born out of a dangerous adventure.

Once it was over and he had the relic back, where would they be? They didn't have anything in common, or any idea if they even did.

Deep inside her heart, where she hid her insecurities and self-loathing, she doubted a powerful, handsome man like him would ever want anything more from a fat girl besides sex.

This mating thing he insisted had happened to him...she wanted to believe it existed. One man, made especially for her —hell yeah, she wanted that to be true.

She'd seen a lot of people who married believing the same thing. Almost as many ended up bitter and alone. A soul mate was a convenient lie.

One she'd used on plenty of brides and grooms in the past.

Real marriage was hard work, not magic.

Not everyone got to find a special someone and at least half of the ones who thought they did were wrong. She was a fool for thinking she was one of the ones who would.

Jakob didn't love her. How could he?

He needed her and had gotten caught up in all of this as much as she had. The trial, ritual and pseudo wedding proved that.

The dread pushed at her again until she scrambled to get out of bed. She slipped out from under Jakob's arms and put her feet on the floor.

She wanted to run, get as far away from him as possible.

Lines wracked his face, worried, even in his sleep. With his wings out like that, he looked like a beautiful fallen angel.

No. Don't think of him now. If she did, she might not have the strength to leave him. She couldn't stay.

The villa sat quiet and Ciara wondered if the other dragons had already left for the States. It was dark outside, so she supposed they could all be sleeping. She had been out for a long time.

She crept through the house, just in case they were about and tried to stop her. She really needed to find some different clothes. This dress was not very good for staying inconspicuous. She didn't even have any shoes.

The last time she tried to escape she tore her feet to shreds. But they'd healed when Jakob blew that green mist over the bite he'd given her in her shoulder.

She placed her hand over the spot. But that made her feel even worse.

She'd be buying a whole set of turtlenecks when she got home.

Her stomach growled, and she decided that grabbing a snack for the road was probably a good idea. She had barely eaten in the past three days, but she couldn't recommend the dragon diet for losing five pounds. Especially because she would definitely gain anything she'd lost back when she got home and spent her evenings with banana splits.

The loaf bread Jakob had found for her when she'd made breakfast was still on the counter. She grabbed it and found a chunk of cheese and some slices of meat in the refrigerator.

Now if she only had a stick and a handkerchief, she could be a well-dressed hobo on her journey to God knows where.

The front door would probably make too much noise, but the hole Jakob and Match had created in the side of the house when they'd fought about her still gaped open. She picked her way through the debris in what looked like the remnants of an office. A suit jacket hung on the back of an executive type chair shoved into one corner. She grabbed it and slipped her arms into it.

It smelled of fresh hay and good and plenty candies. It smelled of Jakob.

She held the jacket to her nose and fought back a killer wave of anxiety.

She was doing the right thing for both of them. She had to believe that.

Jakob would awaken in a few hours and be mad at her for leaving but would probably be on his merry way to his mission of finding the relic soon after.

She shoved the food into her pockets and walked out into the open air. She decided against going toward the town she had found last time. There were woods not far from the other side of the garden. Any other time in her life she would have been nervous about going into a dark forest by herself, but her new abilities, especially the earth element, comforted her. She could call upon the trees and flowers to befriend and protect her.

She imagined an angry apple orchard hurling fruit at any enemies like the ones in the Wizard of Oz.

The only obstacle between her and escape was a pond that contained a very large blue sleeping dragon smack dab in the center of it. She hurried past Ky as quietly and quickly as she could while asking the water to gently rock him.

She was sure she'd been caught when he snorted and snuffled behind her and she broke into a run. Nothing followed her as she dove into the dark forest.

Or had something? She glanced back aware of the feeling of eyes on her and ducked behind a tree.

Ky hadn't moved.

She must have imagined the rustling. Simply because she could now call on the elements didn't mean there wasn't something else out here with her besides earth, wind, water, and fire. The sooner she could get through the woods and find civilization, the better.

Something resembling a path opened up before her. She thanked Mother Nature for showing her a way forward.

Some moonlight shone through the treetops, but there were more dark places than she cared to acknowledge. She had seen the beasts Jakob called the demon dragons appear out of those kinds of shadows.

The sound of twigs breaking behind her sent her running again along the path. She heard nothing else. In fact, the forest had gone too quiet.

Someone or something was definitely in here with her.

She swallowed down the sour taste of fear in the back of her throat and concentrated on the path. A flash of black whipped across the trail in front of her too fast for her eyes to track.

Then she felt a burst of wind when something ran behind her a moment later.

Oh God, she was being hunted.

Hopefully, demon dragons were not as smart as velociraptors.

She heard a screech off to the left and something black and

winged fell from the tree above her. There was more than one.

She was running faster now than she ever had in her entire life. But that wasn't saying much. She was no track star. Working out had never exactly been high on her priority list.

If she survived the night, she was counting this as all the exercise she needed for a month or more. Her heart and lungs were pretty damn mad at her at the moment.

A black, clawed arm reached for her and she threw up a wall of dirt to block it.

Duh. She needed to use her powers. She couldn't afford to stop and close her eyes to concentrate so she hoped she wouldn't screw this up and create more of a barrier for herself.

This next part was going to hurt.

Ciara made herself remember being held in Jakob's arms. The burn of emotion from that memory stretched out all around her and she called upon the ground and trees to form a BBW-sized tunnel she could run through protected.

The forest bent to her will and dirt and branches fused together forming an archway a few feet wide that surrounded her as she ran.

The creatures outside scratched and scrambled at her shield and a too many of their claws managed to poke through.

In minutes she was covered in scratches and she wasn't sure how much longer she could keep running this way. She pressed a hand under her ribs and did her best to breathe through the pain of the stitch forming there.

If she didn't find help or shelter soon, she'd be done for.

The rasps of her heavy breathing made it hard to hear much else, but the whistle of a train somewhere ahead was loud enough to break through. She listened hard but didn't hear the chugga-chugga of the train moving along the tracks. That had to mean there was a station ahead.

If she could only get to that train, maybe she could escape the demon dragons. Or maybe they would attack all of the people on the train. She had to risk it.

One of the demon dragons got wise to her protective barrier and jumped into the trail ahead of her, close enough that she didn't have fast enough reactions to veer away.

Right before her eyes, talons tackled the beast and tossed it aside. They didn't stick around long enough for her to see who it was.

All she knew was that it wasn't Jakob's green scales. The claws had been pitch black.

Were they fighting over her?

The tree line broke a few feet ahead and she barreled out and almost smacked into the metal side of the train. With her last bit of energy, she ran along the track and up to a Soviet era style cement train platform. She climbed up the three metal steps and into the train car, grabbing the sliding door's handle and pulling it shut. The whistle blew again and the train jerked, lurching forward. It took an interminably long time to move past the platform and away from whatever had been chasing and helping her escape. She stared out the small glass window in the door searching for any clue.

There. At the edge of the wood, a man crouched in the remnants of her plant and earth barrier. His clothes were tattered, and she could only just make out his black hair. But his jet-black eyes tracked her.

Who the hell was he?

Whoever he was, he remained in the woods, not following her.

Ciara was still breathing hard and tried her best to get her lungs under control before she entered the passenger car. She pushed the door open and found rows of bench seats, with only a few sleepy riders. She slipped into a seat and glanced around to see if she could figure out where this train was going.

A white placard was screwed into the wall above the windows. It showed a line with periodic dots labeled with words she did not understand. One dot was lit up. The labels appeared to be city names. The last dot on the line was labeled *Praha Hlavni Nadrazi.*

Prague.

But was she going in the right direction? There were only five stops between the dot that was lit up and the end of the line in the direction she hoped she was traveling.

Someone who she assumed must be a train conductor walked toward her down the aisle. Crap. He would want to see her ticket. He stopped at another passenger and Ciara watched him tear off a slip of paper from a pad dangling from the belt at his waist and exchange it for money.

Here goes nothing. She closed her eyes and asked the wind to help her out. She heard a yelp and peeked out of one eye. The train conductor was caught up in a foot-tall swirling dust devil. Oops, too much. She pulled back on the power and used his and the rest of the passengers' distracted state to tear off one of the paper tickets and floated it over to her seat.

The ticket taker pulled himself back together, brushed himself off, and glared at the others who were openly staring at him. Then he made his way over to her. He frowned at her appearance, looking her torn jacket and dress up and down, stopping for an extra second to gawk at her bare feet. *"Bileta, prosim."*

She could only assume he was asking for her ticket. "Sorry, I don't understand Czech. Is this what you want?"

She held the piece of paper, praying it was valid. He punched it with a little hand-held machine and handed it back to her.

Phew.

She spent the next twenty minutes staring at the placard waiting for the dot to change. The next stop closest to Prague lit up. Yes.

A chime and then a female voice came over a crackling loudspeaker four more times in the next hour and a half. She almost had the foreign words memorized by the time they rolled toward the final destination. *"Ukoncete prism, vystup a nasty, Deere se zaviraji."* Then finally, *"Pristi stanice Praha Hlavni Nadrazi."*

Next stop, Prague.

Dawn approached as she made her way out of the already busy train station.

She was here, but what was she going to do now? She didn't have any ID or money. How did she think she was going to get home?

She'd already proven calling home for help was a fruitless endeavor. Maybe she'd just take up residence here and become a homeless person.

She could live in a park and grow her own food. Until the freezing winter came and she froze to death. No, wait. She had fire.

Hmm. This plan was sounding better and better. Even better than going back to America and being a stupid wedding planner again.

She had herself convinced until she was surrounded by a

group of grubby-faced children in clothing more tattered than her own.

A woman stood nearby holding a crying baby. The children all spoke at once, chanting something and making faces at her. They bumped and jostled her, laughing like they were playing a game.

Then in another instant they fled.

A young man in a fancy uniform with a United States of America flag on it walked toward her, scowling at the scamps. "Miss, you need to be careful hanging around *Hlavni Nadrazi*. If you had anything in your pockets, those Romani children have it all now."

"Romani?" She shoved her hands into the pockets of the jacket and came up with nothing but air. They'd stolen her food.

The reality of being homeless in a city like this in a foreign country hit her hard and she started crying.

Dammit.

"You may have heard them referred to as gypsies. They hang around here and a lot of the other touristy areas making their living. Are you okay?"

"No." She sniffled and tried to wipe at her face, but the sleeve of the jacket fell off, the remaining shreds simply giving away.

The young man looked her up and down, but in a much gentler way than the train conductor or anyone in the station had. "I'm a US Marine, ma'am. I work at the embassy here. Do you need assistance?"

Boy, did she ever.

The marine took her on a tram, paying her fair, and escorted her all the way to embassy row. The city was gorgeous, with a giant castle on a hill, a river through the center, covered in ornate bridges.

She wished she could have seen it any other way.

Another time, in another life maybe.

She gave her sob story to a woman whom the marine introduced her too at the embassy, giving only enough details to make the story plausible, and leaving out every bit about dragons, and magic, and falling in love.

Before she knew it, the embassy woman was in tears too. Must be that emotional part of her new-found magic she didn't understand.

They cried together, then the woman got her a meal and some clothes and somehow finagled her onto a military transport back to the US.

She slept the whole way, despite the noise and stares of the military personnel on board with her. When they landed, she didn't feel any more rested than when they'd taken off.

Someone showed her to a phone and she called Wesley.

"Hey, babe. Where you been?" He was as perky as the day she'd left him.

"It's a long story. Do you think you could come get me? I left my car at the Ketcher-Fast wedding."

"Sure. Where are you?"

A four-hour drive away. The Bridezillas of Willingham Weddings were going to have to wait. "Washington DC."

"Jesus. This better be one hell of a story."

She'd have to figure out what to actually tell Wes while she waited for him.

"It is."

One that she wanted to forget as soon as she could.

BURNING DOWN THE HOUSE

*H*e was going to kill her. First, he was going to find her, then he was going to kiss her, then he was going to fuck her three ways to Saturday until she remembered they belonged together, then he was going to kill her.

When Jakob had woken up without Ciara in his arms and found her missing, he'd panicked. But when Ky had helped him track her through the forest and they found evidence of not only her escape from demon dragons, but the scent of a dragon none of them recognized, he'd gone well beyond panic and into weapons of mass destruction mode.

If anything had happened to her, he would tear down the world to get her back or die trying.

They followed the train tracks where Ciara's scent lingered. She wasn't in any of the small towns along the route to Prague. Thankfully, neither was the scent of the unknown dragon.

All Wyverns knew every single dragon in their Wyr. That worried Jakob more than anything else. It was inconceivable to him that there could be a rogue dragon. But if there was one, he would be very dangerous. It would be too coincidental for him to be in the area around Jakob's villa without being involved in all of the problems that had reared their ugly heads in the past week. Whoever he was, he wouldn't be able to hide from them for long, and if this rogue had Ciara, he wouldn't be long for this world.

Ky picked up Ciara's scent again outside the main terminal. He tracked her across the bridge and up the hill to Mala Strana. Prague Castle loomed above them and Jakob swore that when he found Ciara he would take her to the giant hall in the old part of the castle and marry her right.

Her trail landed them standing outside the US Embassy.

"They aren't going to let us in there. None of us even have passports, bro." Shit. Ky was right.

"Speak for yourselves," Cage said. "I've had a passport for years, but not on me. It's not like I flew here commercially."

"Dammit, I'll tear the building down." Jakob paced back and forth in front of the gate.

Match put a hand on Jakob's shoulder and stopped him. "If she went in there, she's safe. Come. Let's find a place where we look a little bit less like a group of terrorists scouting the US Embassy. We'll figure out our next move then."

They walked around the corner and into a little gastropub. Cage grabbed them beers and they sat at a table in the corner.

Before any of them could come up with a suggestion for what to do next, a group of young men entered the bar.

Their loud voices told Jakob that they were probably American tourists, except the one that ordered from the barkeep spoke pretty good Czech. Maybe he lived and worked here.

"No, you guys. I'm telling you she was like a hobo in a ball gown. And the second I told her I was a US Marine she burst into tears," he said as soon as he joined his friends with the beers.

He was in the middle of a story and his friends were enjoying it immensely. "Dude, the sight of you does make most women cry."

The group laughed, but Jakob and the rest of the Wyverns got very quiet. It was more than wishful thinking that they were talking about Ciara.

"What would make you dickheads cry was the sight of her double D's about falling out of that dress. She had curves for miles. I would've escorted her all the way home, if they would let me. If you know what I mean."

If they were talking about his mate, he was going to eat them all for dinner. Two of the men raised their glasses in a toast to the asshole's dirty mind.

One of them prompted their friend to continue the story. "And she said she'd been kidnapped? Who the hell kidnaps an American woman and brings her to the Czech Republic?"

Who else could they possibly be talking about?

"I don't know, man. He must be one sick motherfucker, because she also said he tried to force her to marry him."

Fuck. He'd done no such thing. Had he?

"Jesus Christ, this dude needs to get a life."

"I don't know, maybe we ought to hook him up with your sister Maria."

"Shut up, man."

"So, when can you see her again? Maybe show her a little comfort, Marine style?"

The story teller got series. "Assholes, the lady has been through a serious trauma. Show a little respect."

They didn't know the definition of the word. Jakob's fists clenched. He would teach them.

"In other words, they sent her back to the States, didn't they?"

"On the military transport that left today." The table erupted into laughter again.

Jakob pressed his fists down on the table and slowly stood up. He had no doubt they were talking about Ciara. Had she really said all of those things about him? He had kidnapped her, but this story made it sound like he was a monster.

One of the other Wyverns grabbed at his shirt to stop him, but he was solely focused on the man telling the story, and how he was going to rip his head off.

He walked up to the group without saying a word and lifted the young man up into the air by his collar. "Where is she?"

No one was laughing now. The rest of this young man's comrades stood pushing back their chairs, ready to defend their friend. What he needed now was some of Ciara's calming influence.

"Where. Is. She?" He growled and could feel his dragon pushing toward the surface.

The friends who were so ready to help all took a step back. One of them whispered a series of expletives under his breath.

The man in Jakob's hold grunted. It would probably help if Jakob released his throat. He dropped the man to the bench, watching him gasp for breath. He croaked something out that Jakob couldn't understand.

"What did you say? Tell me where Ciara is."

The man glared up at Jakob. "I said fuck you."

Jakob's talons extended, and his vision sharpened as his eyes and pupils elongated in their dragon form. This little peon would not have a quick death. Jakob would gut him and pull his entrails out slowly until the man told him what he wanted to know.

Cage stepped between Jakob and his prey. "We've learned enough from his story. She went home."

Jakob growled at Cage. Now that he was this close to the man, he scented Ciara all over him. He had touched her. No one touched his mate. She was his.

Cage stepped forward forcing Jakob to back up. He tried to shove Cage out of the way so he could eviscerate his prey. Suddenly, Match and Ky flanked him, creating an immovable wall of dragon warrior. He bared his teeth at them all, showing them just how close he was to shifting.

"These humans do not need to be let in on our ancient secret. Control your temper, Zeleny."

Jakob had already come to blows with Match, and he would do it again.

"Bro, the longer you stand around here pissing in the air, the longer we all have to wait to get to America and find your mate." Ky said the first thing that made any sense to Jakob. He took a deep breath and pushed the dragon back down.

He hurried out of the pub, wanting to take flight immediately. But the city of Prague hadn't seen a dragon flying over it in more than a thousand years. Either they would need to wait until dark or go back out into the countryside before shifting and flying across the ocean to find Ciara.

After a minute he was joined by the rest of the Wyverns. "I managed to talk the soldiers into not reporting that incident. The one who found Ciara took a little extra convincing. He's actually a good kid and just wanted to know she was safe from our resident dickhead over here."

Cage was a smooth talker and had more treasure than the rest of them combined, so he'd probably paid them off. They could have all the gold in his lair and more if it would help him get to Ciara.

But did she even want that?

For the first time since he had taken her, he wasn't sure what to do. She was his mate, but she was also a human and he couldn't force her to be a part of his world.

She had tried to tell him as much before her second seizure. He wouldn't listen. He should have.

Maybe he should just leave her alone, at least for a little while. That idea tore through his gut like St. George's sword. But if it would make her happy to be out of his life, he would suffer.

He had to check on her though, make sure she wasn't in any danger. They were going to America anyway to find the relic. They had no idea where it might be, and the logical place was to start where he'd found it in the first place.

With Ciara.

His Ciara.

Jakob slammed his fist into the nearest wall leaving a good-sized dent in the façade. "I'll go out of my skin if we have to wait until nightfall to shift and fly across the Atlantic. But it'll take just as much time to find an area secluded enough to shift out of sight of the humans."

"Cage and I have been working on a little something, that will help, inspired by your mate." Ky stepped to the side and raised his hands into the air.

The couple of fluffy white clouds dotting the blue sky over Prague gathered, grew, and darkened. Cage grinned and joined Ky. He took in a deep breath and with his exhalation winds whipped through the city. Within a few moments an enormous storm had formed, clouding out the sun.

When the torrential rain started coming down the light of

mid-day turned as dark as midnight. Jakob and Cage were soaked to the bone almost instantly. Ky danced around in the puddles.

The rain around Match evaporated before it hit his skin. "A little something I prepared for the next tempest from your white witch."

The four of them shifted and took to the skies. As soon as they hit the coast, Ky dived and went into the water. He could swim as fast as they could fly. None of them were as strong a flyer as Cage, but with him along they wouldn't need that extra support of the other golds to push them through the jet stream.

Normally, Jakob didn't mind the silence of flight, but today it gave him too much time to think. Had he forced Ciara into this relationship?

He wanted to blame it on the mating, but he was no primitive beast. He lived his entire life without her, without even a clue he would ever find her.

He would have to find a way to live without her again.

If that's what she wanted.

But the way she writhed under him when he'd fucked her, how she came apart in his arms every time he'd been inside of her. At least her body recognized their connection, even if her mind didn't.

She'd agreed to stay the first time he'd asked her. Maybe that had been a lie, something to give her more time to figure out how to escape him.

His senses were all out of whack when it came to her. Maybe he couldn't scent lies or love on her. He'd been wrong on both counts.

In the hours that followed, one moment he was determined to leave her alone, and the next he was convinced he should go after her.

Not since the first days since he'd become Wyvern had he second-guessed himself so much.

Well, he needed to man up. Be the warrior he was trained to be, the dragon he was born to be.

The way his brother Wyverns had banded together almost from the moment this trouble started truly amazed him. He thought he needed to hide his problems from them and prove his worthiness to be Wyvern.

What he really needed to do was learn from those who had been Wyverns longer than he had. He had secluded himself from them, and in the meantime, they had been learning how to work together.

He was afraid they would need that teamwork for whatever chain of events had started with the missing relic.

They approached the eastern seaboard of the United States. With each flap of his wings, the light in Jakob soul shard grew brighter. It had known its mate all along, glowing from the first time he'd laid eyes on her.

He banked, adjusting their flight path toward where he had originally found Ciara. Match and Cage followed him and as soon as they were over land, Ky joined them in the sky again. She wouldn't be in exactly the same place as she was before, but Jakob trusted his instincts to guide him to her.

"Are you sure this is the right direction?" Ky asked. He hesitated as they flew over a part of landmass that hooked into the ocean creating a cape. "Something or someone is pulling me in that direction."

"I'm sure. I don't feel her there. Is it possible this is where the relic is?"

"We should split into two groups. We know that Ciara is

somehow tied to the relic. If we find it, we may also find her and vice versa."

"Agreed. When we are in range, I'll connect with Steele and see if he has found anything."

"I'll do the same with Daxton."

The group split with Ky and Match heading north, while Jakob and Cage flew south.

Even though they had the time change in their favor, the flight had been long and dusk was setting over the land. It helps Jakob to recognize the lights of the city to where he'd first tracked Ciara. He swooped down over the building he kidnapped her from, but he didn't feel her presence there. Where was she?

He opened his senses as wide as he could and felt a glimmer of her not far away. Within a few minutes, he and Cage were perched on top of a building that overlooked where he felt Ciara. It didn't take long before he found her.

His heart practically busted open from beating so hard at the first sight of her. There, a few floors down from the top, he could see her through the window. She was sitting on a couch with a glass of wine in her hand.

He didn't even know she liked wine. He had an extensive cellar filled with vintages from both his Moravian vineyard and Ky's New Zealand one. One more thing he didn't know about her.

He promised himself he was only here to make sure that she was safe. He'd finally decided in the last hour of the flight. But it took everything he had not to cross over and crash through her window.

A moment later, he wasn't sure if he was glad he hadn't or not. She was joined on the couch by another person —a man.

Jakob's vision went green, creating a hazy sight of her hugging this bastard.

Cage shifted away from him on the roof. "Oh shit. Here we go."

Fucking hell, this had to be the boyfriend she had talked about. One more indication to Jakob that she did not want to be with him.

The other man stroked Ciara's hair and she leaned into him.

If he watched this for another minute, he would tear the man in half and take Ciara back to his villa to lock away in his dungeon.

Jakob finally made the right choice. He spread his wings and took to the air.

Cage followed him at a distance, which was a good idea since Jakob needed to kill something.

He opened his mind and searched for Steele. "Tell me you haven't been digging around in this godforsaken land since I sent you over here."

It didn't take Steele long to reply. "No, sir. I haven't found any evidence of a witches' coven, but we have been rooting out more demon dragons than normal."

Jakob hadn't had time to follow-up with Steele and let him know that his theory about Ciara having a coven or other partners in crime had been wrong.

"Good. I'm in the mood for some death and destruction. Show me where we can find some."

"I'm always up for a good demon dragon battle, Zeleny, but shouldn't we meet up with Match and Ky?" Cage flew in a circle around him.

"Go if you want to. I'm happy to do some dirty work on my own."

"By all means, lead the way. It's been too long since I've had the opportunity to let off a little steam."

They followed Steele's directions and didn't have to go far. Steele waited for them in a park maybe a mile from where Ciara lived. He had cleared the area of humans, and the stench of evil would keep more from wanting to come this way.

Jakob would be assigning at least six green dragons on permanent undercover duty to guard Ciara. But first, he would destroy every single one of the little shits he could find in her vicinity and then some.

As if they had been waiting for Jakob to land, a dozen demon dragons rose up out of the shadows the second his feet touched the ground. Excellent. "These are mine."

Jakob tore into the demon dragons like a Viking berserker with fangs and claws. He eviscerated six of them while the others gawked at him. He didn't care. Bring on more.

He got exactly what he wished for.

All of his frustration and anger were channeled into the battle. None even got close to him before he turned them into stains on the ground.

"*Jakob! Look out.*" Both Steele and Cage called out the warning. A mass of demon dragons dropped from the top of a nearby building, through the trees, and tackled him. Five or six of them held him down while two others reached for his soul shard.

A blast of fire threw half of them off of his back and a blast of water took out three more. He looked up to see Match, Ky, Cage, and Steele all joining the fray.

Jakob swung his tail around clobbering the two bastards who had gotten their hands on his shard. They hadn't been able to take it off of him but had lit up with delight, which was completely creepy, when they had touched it. One of them disintegrated into a puff of ash, but the other took off bounding across the park and disappeared into the shadows.

Jakob spotted it again a couple hundred meters away running directly for the building where Ciara lived.

They were going after her.

Over his dead body.

WHAT WERE YOU THINKING?

*C*iara slept the majority of the car ride from Washington DC to home. She still felt like she could sleep for another week. She was groggy enough that Wes suggested he take her straight home instead of stopping to get her car at the wedding hall. Mrs. Moore, the elderly lady who lived across the hall from her had a spare key, so she agreed. Now that she was here and had Wesley Alexander inside her house, she didn't know what to do with herself. Or him.

She putzed about the kitchen for a few minutes before he shooed her away. "Ciara, sweetie pie, go sit on the couch. I'll throw together a quick amuse-bouche and some wine, and you can tell me all about where you've been the past couple of days. Unless you want to go to bed and I'll get out of your hair."

"No, it would be nice to have some company for a while." She didn't know how much she could actually tell him about her insane adventure without sounding like she needed to be sent to the mental hospital. She could probably relate a similar story to what she had told the people at the embassy. They seemed to have bought that, so she would stick with it.

Wesley pulled a couple of glasses and a bottle of wine off the shelf, poured hers and gave her a light shove toward the living room. She curled her legs underneath her on the couch and took a sip of the wine. Then she sat and stared at the wall for a good five minutes.

She may not have even blinked until Wes set a cutting board with slices of avocado, cheese, chunks of rotisserie chicken, and crackers in front of her. It was the most beautiful meal she had ever seen, and it made her burst into tears.

"That's right, honey. Let it all out." He slipped onto the couch next to her and wrapped her up in a big bear hug.

She dreamed more than once of being in Wesley's arms. But she didn't feel a single tingle or butterfly. He was kind and comforting, and she was completely emotionally drained. He stroked her hair while she sniffled, trying to get herself back under control.

No, no. She'd vowed not to sweep her feelings under the emotional rug anymore. She leaned into him and let the tears flow. It felt good to let it all out. She couldn't remember the last time she had cried. Maybe when she'd been a little girl and her father had left.

It didn't take as long as she would've thought to get all cried out. She blew her nose and one of the napkins and grabbed up her glass of wine to wash the taste of salty tears away.

But the wine in her glass had frozen.

Shoot.

"Yeah, mine did that too a minute ago. Also, I think it's snowing in your kitchen, and your ficus is crawling up the side of your wall." Wesley's voice was remarkably calm, and he picked up his own glass swirling the red mass of crystals around and took a sip. "Yum. Wine slushies."

"You are handling this a lot better than I did."

Why wasn't he slowly backing away from her to escape her and the weirdness happening around her?

"There is a lot of bad shit in our world, this isn't one of them. This is kind of amazeballs." He took another sip of his wine slushy and looked at her expectantly. "I could freak out, or I could just wait for you to tell me what's going on."

The entire story from being caught eating leftover wedding cake, being kidnapped and flown across the ocean, learning magic from a witch named Mrs. Bohacek, mating with Jakob, fighting off demon dragons, the challenge to find the ring, getting dragon married, the possessed visions, her escape, the black-eyed man, getting mugged by Gypsy children and saved by a Marine, to him picking her up in Washington poured out of her mouth.

Wes listened to it all, asked clarifying questions, and repeated "literally?" at least half a dozen times.

When she finished, her heart felt a lot lighter. It still hurt, but it didn't feel quite as heavy. "You're not mad about what happened between me and Jakob, are you?"

"Why would I be mad?"

"Because... You and I... I mean, we had a date. We spent half of the last year flirting with each other." With each word that came out of her mouth she turned more and more into a weird awkward teenager. She had plenty of clues that Wesley might not feel the same way about her as she had about him. She had chosen to ignore them, mostly because she'd wanted somebody to want her back.

She could feel the heat in her cheeks and tried to hide behind her glass of wine. Wesley touched her hand and lowered it, so she had to look at him. "I adore you. You're hilarious when you want to be. You don't take bullshit from anyone except your mother, not even the bridezillas—you genuinely care about them. And I like you a lot. But..."

Great. Here came the I like you but speech. Why could it never be the I like your butt speech?

"If I had a choice between you and a sexy ass dragon warrior like what you found, I'd take him to bed too."

Screech. Ciara's brain pulled on the emergency brake cord. No. Seriously? How had she misinterpreted every single goddamn interaction she'd had with Wesley over the past few years?

"Sweetie, I thought you knew. But, I can see from the holy shit look on your face, that you didn't have a clue. So just in case you're still unsure, I like dudes. Like a lot."

Ciara stalled for another minute by shoving three pieces of chicken in her mouth. She chewed, swallowed, chewed some more, all while Wes chuckled at her.

"Nope. Not a single teeny tiny clue." She didn't even feel as smart as a box of rocks. "I seem to have the relationship intelligence of a four-year-old wheel of cheese."

"It's okay. Not everybody's gaydar works. My parents' certainly didn't." They sat together munching on the snacks while Wes let her process this revelation. He'd obviously had the same conversation a time or two. She wouldn't be surprised if she was not the first woman to have a crush on him. He refilled their wine glasses and gave her an expectant look. She blinked at him and then realized he wanted her to slushy-ize his drink again. She laughed and swirled her finger around until his wine was half frozen.

"Here's what I don't get. If this Jakob guy is hot and good

in bed and convinced he's in love with you, what the hell are you doing back here?"

"Don't you see, it could never work between us? He honestly didn't even understand why I was so mad after the mating ritual. There was no way we could form a lifelong loving relationship. It was more like some sort of Stockholm syndrome."

"I'm not buying that. You can't tell me you didn't have any feelings for him. I can tell by the way you talk about him."

So what if she did? She might be new to accepting feelings but having them for someone didn't mean they were in love or that they could have a meaningful relationship. "I'll get over him."

She might've had too much wine, or her stomach was rebelling against the first real food she'd had in a while because when she said those words she wanted to throw up.

"Did we just establish that you're relationship dumb?"

Ciara made a face at him. "I guess so."

"Well, I'm not. I've had hundreds of relationships. Okay, maybe like five. But I make excellent boyfriend material and I know what I'm talking about. So listen close, honey. If you don't get that awesome ass back to Prague and beg for Jakob's forgiveness, on your knees and naked, I will." He waggled his eyebrows at her, but he was serious at least about the part where she needed to get back with Jakob.

"I don't know. We are from such different worlds. I can't pick up and move to Prague. What would I do there? I don't think I'd make a very good housewife."

"That's all a bunch of bullshit. Different worlds, my ass. You just grew a jungle in your kitchen, rivaled Elsa in the do you want to build a snowman department, and invented the best new drink with your mind. All the rest is fluff."

"Your face is fluff." Fear that everything Wesley said was true had her defense mechanisms rising. She gulped the remainder of her wine down. Then she whispered, "what if he doesn't want me back?"

"First off, he does and you will be miserable for the rest of your life if you don't go find that out. But if for some reason he's as relationship stupid as you are and things don't work out, you need to know you're fucking fabulous and you will find a new hottie. I can't guarantee he'll be a dragon, but I know a couple of drag queens."

Fucking fabulous? Was she? Maybe. But she could work on that. "What about Willingham Weddings?"

"You mean what about your mom. That woman needs to get laid worse than anyone I know. A little lickety on her split and she wouldn't be half so cranky all the time."

"Ew." But maybe he was right. Ciara hadn't seen her mother in a serious relationship in twenty years.

"I'd work on that for her, but I don't know any men who like twatwaffles."

Wes had to grab the rest of the napkins and pat up the wine Ciara spewed all over him.

"Sorry about that." She handed him one more napkin for his hair. "If I leave, you'll get stuck with all of my high maintenance accounts."

"I'll be fine. I've already moved up to a level six bridezilla slayer. Besides, it's all practice for when I start getting us the gay weddings. You haven't seen a bridezilla until you've met the Queen marrying his queen."

Was she really going to do this? She couldn't. She had to. She really was going to throw up.

"Uh, Ciara. I know you said your dragon was super sexy. But that guy looks more like Steve Buscemi as a snake."

Wesley's eyes went as wide as the windows.

Oh no. Ciara slowly turned to see what had scared Wesley. Standing on her small porch was a demon dragon.

She thrust her hand open palm at the monster and blew it tumbling over the side of her porch. Three more appeared out of the shadows.

"Wesley, grab the phone, go to the bathroom and turn on all of the lights, and then call 911. I will keep them at bay as long as I possibly can."

"Shit, shit, shit. That's not your boyfriend is it?"

"No. Go, quickly." When he hesitated, Ciara use the same trick of the wind to lift him bodily off the couch and shoved him toward the bedroom. "Remember, turn on all the lights. They come out of the shadows."

Wes grabbed the phone, stared at it and shook it. "There's no signal."

"Stand on the bathtub and hold the shower curtain rod. You should be able to get one bar."

The demon dragons rattled the sliding glass door. She didn't think they understood how to open it. But just to be safe, she encased the door in a block of ice. It would be impossible to slide it open now.

One of the creatures rolled its head and blew a stream of fire at the ice, melting her handiwork almost instantly. Then it whipped its tail around and shattered the glass.

Fuck three ducks. Think, think. What did she know how to do to defend herself and Wesley? She couldn't run. A dirt barrier would not protect her for long, and now that they had made it inside she didn't know if she could focus her command over the wind to do anything but toss them around the room. If she used fire, she might burn the entire apartment complex down, and they had already shown they weren't bothered by ice.

That was everything she knew how to do.

Ciara backed away, retreating into the plants that had grown up all around her kitchen. She imagined a whip in her mind and a spiky vine lashed out at the nearest demon dragon. It caught the thing in the face, cutting it, but that only made it mad.

"You come. We not hurt." A crackling voice came from one of the demon dragon's mouths.

She hadn't realized they could talk. The speech was stilted and basic. Were they stupid? Maybe she could just talk them into going and leaving her alone. "No. You go."

The two uninjured ones glanced at each other as if they were considering doing what she told them to. "No. You come."

They definitely weren't smart, but she didn't think she could fool them. Maybe she could stall them long enough for the police and their guns to get here. Hopefully, guns worked as a weapon against demon dragons.

Who she really needed was Sam and Dean Winchester.

Scratch that. She needed Jakob.

"Where do you want to take me?"

"AllFather."

"Who is AllFather?"

"AllFather AllFather." They didn't have a whole lot of inflection, but she could tell that one thought she was as stupid as she thought he was. She wanted to ask what the AllFather was too, but she'd probably get the exact same response.

"Where is this AllFather?" This was working. She'd held

them off for a full thirty-seven seconds. How fast were first responders?

The demon dragon who had been answering her questions snarled as if he'd had enough talking. "Hell."

Oh, hell no.

The demon dragons advanced, even the one with the cuts on its face. She sure as hell hoped Wesley had been able to get through to 911.

Ciara needed to come up with a plan and quick. She grabbed a knife from the butcher block and held it out. God, she hoped this did not come down to hand-to-hand combat. She waved the knife at them. It didn't stop them even a little bit. She switched from holding the knife handle like she was going to chop up a grilled cheese sandwich and flipped it, so she fisted the handle, blade down. She'd taken a self-defense class once, kidding, she'd seen one advertised on TV. She did remember though that knife was more powerful and useful in downward stabbing motion then trying to use it like a sword.

She might not be able to throw the demon dragons out the window with her wind, but she could use it to throw things at them. A lamp flew across the room and smacked the bleeding one in the head. He shook his head and kept advancing on her. She threw a lot more at them, books, her TV, snowballs. It didn't stop them even a little bit. She needed a better plan.

What would Jakob do?

Thrash them with his tail. She didn't have one of those. He'd slash their throats with his claws. They would need to be a lot closer to her for that and she didn't want them to be. Bury them in dirt.

All she had were her potted plants and the ground was eight stories below. She had to try anyway.

A fountain of soil spurted in through her broken door and gathered at the demon dragons' feet.

"Come on, come on." She searched deep inside her heart for the strongest emotions in there that she could find. Every single one of them had to do with Jakob. Only this time when she pulled them up they didn't hurt.

The stream of earth thickened and began to avalanche into her living room.

The demon dragons clawed at the dirt and screeched at her.

She called all of the roots out of the tiles, walls, floor, and ceiling from every apartment in the building. They grew hard like stone, encasing the demon dragons inside.

She had them.

She was feeling pretty damn proud of herself, and almost ready to call Wes back out of the bathroom.

That's when something much bigger with giant talons plunked down on her back porch. It was so dark outside now that she couldn't see what it was. But the weight of it shook her building.

If it tried to come inside, she was toast.

SAVE ME

*J*akob followed the demon dragon down the street. The one turned to many as it called its brethren to rise. First two, then ten. More and more formed out of the shadows until a river of them were flowing toward Ciara. Where the fuck were they all coming from and why were they here and now?

It had to be connected to Ciara and the relic. The bastards had never shown any interest in a single human being before. They had only ever been bent on causing plagues and spreading death. They'd brought the black death to Europe, Ebola to Africa, SARS to Asia, and H1N1 around the world. Each outbreak had been stopped from becoming a species annihilator by the dragon warriors.

He and every other dragon ever born had rooted them out, usually one by one, and destroyed them. To see this many gathered together twice in a lifetime was more than a little scary. But for them to be fixated on one human didn't make sense.

The warriors were missing vital clues, and he didn't have

time to hunt them down. He was too busy hunting demon dragons.

Jakob slashed and destroyed them from the back of the newly formed horde, but as soon as he killed one, two more appeared to take its place.

He had to get ahead of them and warn Ciara. Get her out of there and to safety. Preferably back to his villa where he would build a brand new, high-tech safe room, hidden in an underground bunker, that only he knew the location of and the combination. He would hide her away there forever.

Except she would kill him for it. He would enjoy every second of that, and the make-up sex to be had once he rid the world of every last demon dragon.

They were falling fast. He was taking them out two or three at a time. It wasn't enough. As a highly-trained warrior, he knew better than to use only his claws, tail, and fangs to fight his enemy. Use your head, asshat.

They couldn't fly, but he could. If only he had fire. As soon as he thought it, dragon's fire spewed down upon them.

Match swooped in over the horde and took out a dozen right down the middle. The remaining right flank of them froze in their tracks, encased in blocks of ice by Ky which he then shattered into hundreds of chunks of demon-cicles.

Jakob shouted his thanks and jumped into the air over the battle. He put on a burst of speed, needing more than his own wings were capable of doing. He flew faster than ever and still hadn't caught up to the front of the pack.

A warm wind blew him from behind. *"Go to her brother. Save your white witch. Save your mate. We'll protect the rest of the humans from here."*

Jakob sped ahead, cracking more skulls with his tail as he

flew overhead. He spotted Ciara's apartment instantly by the broken glass door.

Fuck. Three demon dragons were inside, and he didn't fucking fuckity fuck fit through that doorway. He wouldn't even fit inside her apartment. Not as a dragon.

His only weapon as a man was his command of earth, and they were a hundred meters up from the ground. Ciara had cleverly brought a good metric ton of earth up, but much more and her floor would collapse.

He landed on the small wooden porch and had to dig his claws into the brick of the building to keep it from collapsing under him. Inside, she had the demon dragons encased in what looked like termite hills, but they were already breaking free. If he shifted now, his human form would be too vulnerable to do any good. He could protect Ciara for no more than a few minutes before the demon dragons would slice through that weak form.

But he couldn't stand out here with his thumb up his ass watching as they attacked her.

He roared and ripped the frame of the sliding glass doors out of the side of the building, tossing it to the ground. That garnered him only a little more than a glance from one of the demon dragons. They knew they were safe from him inside this tiny space.

But the look of relief on Ciara's face made the effort worth it. Her energy was flagging, he could see it in the exhaustion written all over her face and the way she supported herself against the kitchen counter. Poor thing had been going like a damned Energizer bunny hopped up on meth for days. He hadn't given her half a chance to rest. He'd barely fed her. If they made it out of here alive, he swore he'd take better care of her, feeding her gourmet meals in bed if she wanted.

Her breathing was labored, and her outstretched arms shook like blades of grass in the wind. She wasn't used to battling these bastards or even wielding her magic, and didn't know how to conserve her energy. If he didn't do something soon, her reserves would be exhausted.

You are doing great, my love. I am here for you. We just need a plan to get you out of here.

She gave one quick shake of her head and looked toward a closed door on the side of the room. "I can't leave. My friend Wes is hiding in the bathroom."

One of the demon dragons broke free from his dirt bonds and advanced on her. Jakob swiped the one part of his anatomy that he could get into the apartment, his tail, trying to reach it. The demon dragon jumped to the ceiling to avoid the dangerous spikes, realizing when it did, that Jakob couldn't get to it. It landed back on the floor and turned its back on him, stalking toward Ciara.

Christ. He had made the situation worse.

Ciara pulled a spray nozzle from the sink and shot a steady stream of water, pumped up by her command of the element to the level of a fireman's hose. That deterred the demon dragon for only a moment, until it pushed forward through the water, inching closer to her.

Another beast broke free and she was forced to move the spray back and forth between the two of them, only managing to irritate them.

God dammit. He had to figure out a way to get the focus off of her and back to him. They could easily destroy him if he shifted back to a man, but why would they? He'd be no threat.

He scratched and yanked out more pieces of the wall, trying to get to her. An older woman came to the window above and stuck her head out. "Shut up, down there. You'll wake the —" Her eyes went as wide as the rollers in her hair when she saw Jakob clawing at the side of the building. He roared at her and she disappeared back into her apartment. If he was lucky, she would think this had all been a dream. But to get to Ciara, he would need to destroy that woman's apartment too. That would be hard to explain away.

"Jakob. Help me." The third demon dragon had freed itself and the three of them now had Ciara penned in the kitchen. She had climbed up on top of the counter with the help of the plants growing up the walls.

Why weren't they just attacking her? What were they waiting for?

The answer to that would be the key to saving her.

"Stop fight. Dragon not save you. Come now, witch." One of them screeched and growled words at her.

Holy shit holes. They weren't out to kill her. They wanted her to come with them for some reason.

He needed to find something they wanted more to get them away from her. He didn't even know until tonight that demon dragons wanted anything. They were mindless monsters.

Someone or something else had to be pulling their strings. That was some powerful dark magic.

One lunged for her and Jakob pulled up a wave of the earth inside her apartment to push it back. He used the momentum of that to propel the demon dragon hard into the wall, and then he gathered the rest of the dirt and tossed it and the demon dragon over the side of the building. It fell those eight stories, flapping its useless wings and crashed into the ground below

One down, two to go. Except in watching that bastard fall to its death, he'd seen the horde he'd had overtaken was now approaching the building. The Wyverns, Steele, and a young red dragon who must be Daxton were taking them out one by one. But there were so many that their efforts were more like thinning a herd, not sending them all off to slaughter.

He had maybe three minutes before they reached her building and began the climb up.

Think, for fuck sake. What did these demon dragons want, besides Ciara?

The only other thing he'd ever seen any of them tried to get, was his soul shard. He had no idea why they would want it, but twice in as many days they had tried to nab it off his neck. One of the two pieces of shit left in Ciara's apartment had gripped it in its very paws, and instantly seemed to know exactly where she was.

If their mission from God knows who was to capture Ciara and get his soul shard, maybe, just maybe they would be dumb enough to turn their attention to him. They would be more likely to attack if he was less of a threat.

With so many demon dragons around, and Ciara's life in danger, it was difficult to push his dragon back down. The shift took longer than he wanted it to. He could hear the horde and the ensuing battle getting closer.

He prayed to the First Dragon that this would work. *Please, help me save her.*

He finally shifted into his human form and gripped his soul shard in his fist. He knew dragons who had taken their shards off and had lost their ability to shift along with it. He never had taken his off.

He yanked on the cord, breaking it free from his neck. His heart stuttered and for a second, he thought he might fall to his knees from the sensation that shot through his body. He gritted his teeth and pushed through the waves of weakness washing over him.

He wrapped the remnants of the cord around his fingers, held his hand aloft, and dropped the shard to dangle from his hand. "Hey assholes, look what I have for you."

The two demon dragons' heads snapped around and stared at him. The soul shard shined like a beacon, green light filling the apartment and the night sky.

"Yeah, that's right. Come and get it." Behind them, he could see Ciara shaking her head and reaching her hand out for him.

Jakob's energy drained and his vision blackened. He hadn't expected that. No other dragons had reported something like this happening to them. But then again, he had never heard of anyone else's soul shard glowing or helping them find a mate. This kind of information would've been nice to have been passed down through the generations. Not that he had another plan to distract the demon dragons, even if he had known.

He called upon his reserves to give him a small partial shift, turning his hands into claws and talons. The longer he could defend himself, the more time it gave Ciara to get to her friend and get away. That little cocksucker had better take care of her.

"Go, Ciara. Run. Get your friend and get out of here." Jakob's knees buckled underneath him and he fell to the wooden slats of the porch. The structure wavered under the weight of his fall, and the damage he had done to it.

"No, I won't leave you. No way. I can't. I love you, you asshat."

The words filled his heart with hope and joy. He thought her lost to him forever, and even if he only lived a few more minutes, he would die a happy man knowing she'd been with him at the end. But he would haunt her from the afterlife if she put herself in danger now. "The others are coming. They will save you."

The two demon dragons snarled and continued their approach. They were rightfully cautious of him, but he could see in their eyes that they understood probably better than he had that any defense he put up would be no more than that of a newborn youngling. He shook the ends of the cord, swinging the shard back and forth in front of their eyes.

"Here, demon, demon, demon. Here, demon, demon. Come and get it." His voice came out raspy and weak, but it got the point across. He had the shard, and it was theirs for the taking.

Of course, he had no intention of actually letting them get it. He had saved a tiny bit of strength, fueled by the memory of his first kiss with Ciara, the first time he'd been inside of her, the first time he'd made her come, and her final words to him. I love you. Technically, her last words were you asshat, and even those words gave him the strength that he needed.

With the demon dragons half a meter in front of him, he called out an ancient war cry and rose to his feet thrusting his talons through one of them and throwing his soul shard, with all of his might across the room to Ciara.

He heard her wail as the final demon dragon attacked him using its fangs and claws to tear into him.

It was a good death, even though he hated to leave her. It was with the knowledge that in the end, he had finally given her his soul. It had always been hers anyway.

READ MY LIPS

*C*iara picked a damned fine time to decide she was in love. Maybe she had known it all along, she was sure that was what she was denying herself when she left Jakob in the Czech Republic. But even that felt nothing like the joy shredding her from the inside out right now.

Jakob had come for her. He was here, and he was dying right in front of her eyes.

Fuck that.

No way, José.

Nuh-uh. Not gonna happen.

Read my lips. No new taxes.

Fire, wind, water, and white light swirled around her. The only element missing was earth. Jakob was her world, her connection to mother nature, herself. Without him, she would never be whole.

He had given himself to her, mind, body, and soul, never questioning that they belonged together. She was the one who had never been able to see it, when the one thing she wanted more than anything in her whole life, real true love, had been given to her freely.

She'd been too scared to reach out and take it. She'd learned over the years that love offered meant that it came with obligation and compulsion. It wasn't free and what was owed in return for it was more than she had ever been able to give, even as hard as she had tried. Somewhere along the way, she'd given up, and sheltered her battered heart, cutting it off from all the commotion. If she didn't have to feel, then it wouldn't hurt.

She taught herself to be miserable and to pretend that it didn't matter. But it had. More than she had ever understood, or ever admitted. She wanted connection, and she wanted love. It was what made her human.

The relic, the white witch, and the magic of the mating had thrown them together. But it had been Jakob who had shown her what love could be like.

It was rough around the edges, like an unpolished diamond, and she would not have it any other way.

It was too precious for her to lose it now.

Ciara gathered strength from her conviction, multiplying it by touching it with love. The magic gathered around her, sparking through the air.

She rose up off the ground and walked on the wind, her hair whipping all around her. Thunder and lightning crackled around her. She used the electricity in the air to fuel her fire, then she shot it toward the black beast still hulking over Jakob's body. Its skin, then the rest of it, burned so hot in a blue flame that not even ash or the telltale inky stain remained. She blocked Jakob from the burning with a bubble of cool mist around him.

Now that her enemy was vanquished, she moved toward

her love. But she was not yet allowed to reach him. An onslaught of demon dragons poured in through the side of the apartment building, like a stream of black scarabs focused on their next meal of human flesh. They disregarded Jakob and that spiked her fear that he was truly dead already. Instead, they angled toward her in a dark wall that threatened to suffocate her.

But she was done with fear. Done with the powerlessness of being a victim. The innermost core of her being was naked for all the world to see, and she reveled in the sensation.

Everything she never thought she could do, all the hopes and dreams that had been dashed by self-doubt and recriminations, each failed attempt to be what she wasn't burned up and washed away in the torrent of her true self.

These monsters could tear, bite, and try to harm her, but she would not be defeated.

Power flowed through her, wanting to burst out of her body.

One of the beasts with a much bigger body and wings shoved some of the others aside and reached for the soul shard Jakob had tossed across the room. She hadn't even tried to catch it, solely focused on him. Now, there was no fucking way she was letting any other being in the universe touch that last vestige of him.

She shoved the wall of demon dragons back with a storm of fire and ice. They screamed and screeched, fizzled and popped out of existence, blackening her room with their deaths.

She struck down the larger demon dragon just as he grasped Jakob's soul shard by the cord. She threw him up against the wall and pinned them there.

Another wave of demon dragons crashed in through the

hole in her wall and she had to divide her attention. With one hand she held the horde at bay and with the other dragged her prisoner across the ceiling and to her.

She prepared a sharp sword of ice to run him through. The bastard dangled from the ceiling above her and she looked into familiar jet-black eyes. What the hell?

It startled her so bad that she lost control and dropped him to the floor. He landed with an umph and the shard skittered across the floor. The two glanced at each other, to the shard, and back.

They both scrambled for it. Ciara snagged it a millisecond before he got there.

Old black eyes frowned at her, if that's what she could call the grimace on his dragon-like face. *You win this round, witch. I relinquished the prize to you. But I will be back, and you owe me one.*

He spread his wings and took three running steps across the room and out the window into the air, taking the mass of demon dragons she'd been holding at bay with him, swiping them up in his wings like dust in a pan. He caught an air current and flew up while the remainder of her enemies fell to the ground.

She followed him as far as her now rickety porch to ensure that no more would enter her domain. Snort laugh. Her destroyed apartment was far from a castle on a hill, but it contained a treasure far greater than any gold or silver.

Ciara glanced down to the yard and saw the other dragons she had come to know, and another green, and a new red one battling on her front lawn. It looked like a scene out of a fantasy video game. All they needed were a few knights in shining armor with clanking swords to complete the look. There were still more demon dragons than warriors, but no more climbed up the walls of her building and their numbers were declining as she watched. The warriors seemed to have the horde under control for now.

With no new imminent danger, she rushed back and slid on her knees to Jakob's side.

His blood was everywhere, and his skin was ashen. "No, no, no. Please don't be dead." She shook his shoulder and placed one hand on his cheek. She knew nothing about death and had no idea if it should still feel warm like it did or not. "Jakob, if you're still in there. Hold on. Please."

She choked the words out but didn't know what else she could do to save him. Was there such a thing as a dragon doctor or a dragon emergency room?

She pressed a soft kiss to his lips and then turned her head to see if she could feel any breath on her cheek. A small moan and breath of air passed from between his lips. It was the most beautiful sound she'd ever heard. He scrunched one eye like he had nothing more than a headache and the other blinked open. "Am I dead? Are you my angel come to take me to the afterlife?"

Ciara pressed her lips to his again, wanting to feel his breath for herself. "No, my beautiful dumbass. You're not dead and you better not even think about dying on me now."

"No promises," he croaked out.

He might be conscious, but he wasn't out of danger. She'd heard dying people needed something to live for. "What if I make you one?"

He closed his eyes and grimaced. "Hit me with it, but not too hard. I might break."

"I, Ciara Mosley-Willingham, take you, Jakob Zeleny, as my lawfully wedded husband. I do promise to love you for richer or for poorer, through sickness and in health, as long as we both shall live."

Jakob didn't say anything, and his eyes remained closed.

Ciara's heart stopped, waiting, waiting. Her lungs burned, her skin tingled, and her eyes filled with tears.

He sighed softly. "Aren't I supposed to give you a ring and a kiss now?"

She laughed and cried at the same time, choking over her own words. "You already did."

A ring and a kiss that she'd denied, almost lost, and wanted more than anything now.

His breath came out ragged. "I wasn't sure you wanted to keep them."

"I do. They're mine, just like you are." She was never letting any of this go ever again.

"About time you figured that out." He coughed, blood coming out of his mouth.

"Oh, Jakob. You're hurt really badly. I don't know what to do to help. The other dragons are all still fighting the demon dragons." All she'd ever had was basic babysitter's first-aid. She had never had to use it on anything more than her own scraped knee.

He groaned trying to get words out. He coughed again and rasped his request. "My soul shard. Do you have it?"

She plucked the shard up from where she had dropped it when she knelt beside him. "Yes, right here. Should I put it back on you? Will that help?"

Jakob slowly opened his eyes again, the light there fading so rapidly. He lifted his hand, she didn't know how, and she pressed the shard to his palm. He wrapped his hand around both it and her fingers.

"Put it on."

She moved their hands toward his neck, but he resisted. "No. You put it on. Wear it. It belongs to you. My soul belongs to you."

His hand dropped, and his eyes fluttered shut. Ciara scrambled to tie the cord around her neck so that he could see his last wish fulfilled. She grabbed his hand back up and pressed it against her chest.

"I have it, Jakob. I have it. Your soul is mine. Forever."

But he was gone.

The shard burned against her skin, the green light igniting her, him, and the entire world.

Fear and anxiety, lust and need, sadness, contentment, and dare she say happiness all flowed over, around, and through her. She wanted to cry and laugh and throw up and dance all at the same time.

Gah. It was too much. It wasn't enough.

The dam she'd put up long ago to hold back all of her emotions broke and the world exploded.

The light reached inside of Ciara and sparked and flickered into red flame, blue mist, golden wisps of wind, and the green spark of life itself. It flickered across her body, pooling in her heart and combining the colors into the purest of white hot love.

She arched her back, letting the power flow through her, over her, and out into Jakob. Everywhere the white magic swirled, his body was knit back together. Fire cauterized his wounds, water and ice cooled them. The wind whipped the magic across his body and the lush green life force inside of him grew and grew until he sucked in a great breath. The magic of love surrounded him, mixing with Ciara's until they both overflowed with it.

Jakob's eyes flew open and he caught Ciara's hand in his.

Their eyes met, and they gazed at each other in wonder and awe.

The light around them slowly faded, some into Jakob's chest and the rest into Ciara's womb.

She wrapped her arms around him and swore she'd never let go.

Uh, are we interrupting something. Want us to come back later, lovebirds? Cage landed in the hole in the wall, shifted into his cocky ass human form and sauntered into her disaster of a living room.

Match and another red dragon followed, doing the same, and then Ky and a green dragon. Ky looked around at the overturned furniture, the black stains all over the room, and at the dried blood covering Jakob. "Bro, she's not much of a housekeeper. You should think about getting a maid to help out around here, *Wahine.*"

Ciara squirted him in the face with water. He laughed and winked at her.

"Wyvern, are you injured? Do you need dragon's breath?" Steele asked.

"Umm. Ew." The warriors all assumed fighting stances again and turned toward the door on the side of the room. Wesley stood in the doorway.

"Whoa, guys. This is my friend Wes. Wes, welcome to DragonCon."

STRONGER TOGETHER

*C*iara's love may have healed Jakob's injuries, but he was not back to one hundred percent. If he were, he would have picked up this Wesley character and tossed him out the window. Jealousy was a particularly strong attribute in green dragons. Right now, he didn't want any other man or dragon even looking in her direction, much less talking with and touching her.

"Jakob, stop with the growling. Wes is my friend. Nothing more."

"Then why is he touching you?" Maybe he did have the strength to toss the pecker overboard. Every second Wes had his arm around Ciara, Jakob felt stronger and stronger.

Ciara frowned at him and narrowed her eyes into a glare.

"Because we have all been through a very big ordeal and need comforting."

Jakob grabbed her hand and pulled her into his lap. "I will comfort you."

"I mean, I'll take a hug from him." Wes opened his arms and waved Jakob into them.

Jakob just stared at him.

"Okay, your loss. I'm an excellent hugger. Ask Ciara."

Wesley was lucky Jakob was not a red dragon. Because he would be toast right now.

It was far too long before Jakob could have Ciara all to himself again. Wes had managed to get through to the emergency services and a whole squadron of police cars and fire trucks surrounded her building. Cage, the Great Convincer, somehow managed to make them all think that the blackened interior, the hole in the side of the building, and the stains all over the lawn were from a kitchen fire. In fact, he had the building superintendent apologizing all over himself for not noticing such shoddy work and the possibility of a dangerous situation.

Whatever. Jakob would pay what it took to either repair the building or buy it outright. It wasn't like Ciara needed to live here anymore. As soon as he could, he would be taking her back to the Czech Republic. He just hadn't told her that yet.

Later.

After a lot of hot makeup sex. He was really looking forward to makeup sex.

Steele never strayed far from Jakob's side. He'd insisted on giving Jakob a good dose of dragon's breath in case he still had any lingering injuries. Even when Jakob had shooed him away to heal the other Wyverns and Dax's wounds, his second in command continued to check on him.

When the police and fire departments finally called it quits for the night, the sun was already rising. Wesley finally proved himself useful and got them rooms at a local hotel that Ciara said they booked often enough for weddings that he should tell them they owed her a favor.

When they arrived at the hotel and Steele tried to escort him and Ciara to their room, Jakob had had enough. He sent Ciara ahead and pulled Steele aside.

"What's going on with you? I'm pretty sure I don't need a babysitter in the bedroom tonight."

Steele rolled his neck and leaned back against the hallway wall, propping one foot up against it. "Sorry, man. It's just no second has ever lost their Wyvern. I'm not even in my prime yet. I don't know how to lead a Wyr, I was pretty damn sure tonight that I was going to have to. You scared the shit out of me, dying like that."

Jakob clapped Steele on the arm. "I was only dead for like a second. It's fine."

He figured it must be something like that. They were both young to be leaders of the Green Dragons and there was a lot of pressure to be good at it. But it was pressure that Jakob needed to shoulder, not Steele. "You look like you could use a vacation. I'm putting you on a week's leave."

"No, I'm fine."

"I am your Wyvern, and you will do as you are commanded. Understood?"

Steele raised an eyebrow but nodded. "Understood."

"You look like you could use a good lay. Make that happen on your leave."

Steele laughed and saluted. "Yes, sir."

"Good. Orders effective immediately. Get the hell out of here." Steele glanced at the door Ciara had disappeared into, gave a curt nod, and trotted down the hall.

Thank God.

Jakob pushed into the room and found Ciara on the phone ordering room service. "Yes, I realize it's 7 o'clock in the morning but I still want two cheeseburgers. And throw a couple fried eggs on top. And cheese. And French fries and chocolate cake."

She hung up the phone and fell back on the bed. "It'll be here in half an hour. If I don't make it that long, then wake me up. I'm starving."

He needed much more than half an hour to do all the things he wanted to do to her. But he supposed they would need some sustenance to keep their energy up. "I can think of a few things to keep you awake for the next thirty minutes."

Jakob peeled off his shirt and tossed it directly into the trashcan. He glanced at Ciara hoping she was undressing as well. She propped herself up on one elbow on the bed wide-eyed, simply staring at him.

"What? Do I still have blood on me somewhere?" Ciara had insisted on cleaning him up with a warm soapy washcloth while they waited for the police and firemen to finish their business. But his guts had been spilled out all over the place, so there was a good chance she'd missed something.

"No. It's just... you're so fucking hot. I could stay here and look at you all day."

"While I'm flattered, that doesn't sound like as much fun as what I had in mind." And that required for them both to be naked.

"Oh, really? I can't imagine anything more fun than me getting to explore every nook and cranny of your body."

Jakob crawled onto the bed, rolling her on her back and pinning her under him. God, how he loved the feeling of having her beneath him.

"Only after I get to explore all of your nooks and crannies with my tongue."

"You're a dirty dragon."

"You would know." She giggled, and he inhaled her

laughter into his mouth along with her kiss. He took his damn sweet time kissing her, licking her lips, sucking her tongue into his mouth, pushing his into hers rhythmically, mimicking what his cock was going to do to her pussy later. She moaned and pushed her hands into his hair, kissing him back with as much ferocity. He'd always taken charge, because he knew she liked that, liked giving over her power and submitting to him. But it would be a lot of fun to put her on top. Let her decide what she wanted him to do to her, for her. He slid his hand up under her shirt and found her nipple. He pinched it through her bra loving the sound of her whimpers as he did.

"I'm going to fuck these lush tits of yours later, come all over them."

"Mmm, we should have grabbed my toy chest when we were at my apartment. I have a pair of nipple clamps connected with the chain that would have looked great wrapped around your cock."

Holy hell. "I'll just have to buy you a whole new toy chest. Until then we'll make do with fingers and tongues."

He traced his fingers down her chest across her soft belly and under the waistband of her pants. His fingers skimmed the lace of her panties. "I thought I told you not to wear these."

He slipped his hand beneath them and pushed a finger into her wet heat.

"Ooh, yes, right there." She squirmed, doing her best to ride his fingers. "If you don't want them on me, you'll just have to take them off."

Jakob ripped her pants and underwear down her legs and threw the remnants over his shoulder. "Spread your legs for me, Ciara."

She didn't have to be told twice. She lifted her knees and

opened her thighs, exposing her pretty pink pussy. First, he would make her come with his hand and then he would make her come again as he lapped up all of her cream. He wanted to hear her cry his name. And even more he wanted to hear those three little words from her as he buried himself deep inside of her.

He pushed two fingers into her, stretching her and feeling her inner walls clench around him. He pressed his thumb against her clit and squeezed her rhythmically.

"Oh God, Jakob." She threw her head back and her arms over her head gripping the pillows in her fists.

She was already so wet that his hand was soaked. He drew some of the liquid out of her and pulled it down coating her little tight pucker. He did that two more times until her own juices lubricated her asshole. Then he slowly pushed a finger into her there too. He worked a finger in and out of her ass as two fingers of the other hand thrust into her pussy.

"Jakob. Jakob," she moaned exactly what he wanted to hear. "That's going to make me come so hard. Ooh. Yes. Yes."

A knock sounded on the door, two fast raps.

"Oh no. The food," she panted the words between gulps of air.

"Tell them you're coming, Ciara."

He fingered her holes relentlessly and finally added his thumb back into the mix, swiping over her clit, fast and hard.

The knock sounded again along with a call through the door. "Room service."

"Tell them you're coming, my love. Now."

Her body clenched and jerked, her orgasm hitting her hard. "I, I, I'm coming. I'm coming."

Her muscles squeezed his fingers as she exploded, but he didn't let up. "Give me more, Ciara. You're not done yet."

Her words had turned to primitive guttural sounds. Her head thrashed back and forth and her back arched as her body came, as he drew the orgasm out.

She finally collapsed onto the bed, periodically moaning as another and another pulse gripped her. Jakob didn't pull his fingers out until he was sure her body was replete.

He wiped the fingers that had been in her pussy across her lips and then kissed her, letting them both taste her. She bit at his lip and he nipped her back.

"Hungry, darling?"

"Always." She had a sloppy grin on her face that he loved.

"Then let's eat." Jakob quickly washed his hands and opened the door to retrieve the food. The tray had been left at the door, the delivery person long since fled.

He'd tip the staff big later for their trouble.

By the time he got the tray back into the room, Ciara was snoring softly. He couldn't imagine how tired she was. Probably twice as tired as he was, and he was near dead on his feet.

He couldn't decide whether he should let her sleep or wake her up and feed her. She'd been pretty adamant about getting these burgers, so he figured she wanted them badly enough that she wouldn't be mad if he woke her up.

He grabbed a French fry and painted her lips with it. She licked the salt away and her eyes popped open. "Mmm. That's not what I thought that was."

"And you say I'm the dirty one."

She licked the fry and took a bite out of it. If Jakob though his cock was hard before, he was wrong. Hard was nothing compared to the stone rod pressing against his zipper watching her eat.

He'd never wanted to be a French fry so badly in his life.

Ciara grinned, sat up, and kissed him. Then she rolled her

bare ass across the covers and pulled the top off the other tray. She grabbed the cheeseburger and took an enormous bite out it. The yolk from the fried egg on top ran down her chin.

"Fuck, my love. You could make eating into a porno. Another few minutes of watching you eat and I'm going to come in my pants."

She licked her lips, dipping her tongue down to catch the dribble of egg and waggled her eyebrow at him.

That was all he could take. He pushed her back on the bed and licked that exact same spot. She squealed and giggled but didn't let go of her cheeseburger for one second. In fact, she took another bite and then turned the sandwich and gave him a bite.

"That's all you're getting for now, dragon. I ordered you your own. Go eat it."

He snagged another quick bite of hers just to get a rise out of her. Then he let her up and got his own food.

Even though he was still harder than was comfortable, they took a nap after they ate. But they saved the chocolate cake for later.

He planned to smear chocolate icing all over her and then lick it off. He was sweet on her after all.

Then he was going to smear it all over himself and let her do the same.

LOVE AND OTHER DRUGS

iara woke up hours later, with Jakob's arms and legs wrapped around her. It was right where she wanted to be.

And it felt so damn good to finally admit that. Some real crazy shit had gone down in the past five days. Was it really only five days?

It felt like a lifetime.

Luckily, that's what she had to look forward to. A lifetime with Jakob.

She had no doubt that it was not always going to be easy. He did love to be an asshat, and she was definitely a witch, the bad kind not the good kind, on occasion.

They would probably fight, there would probably be tears, there would definitely be items thrown and broken, and she envisioned more than one wall in their house needing to be repaired. They should probably put a construction crew on retainer.

And it was all because he loved her, and she loved him.

She was more than a little worried about the future,

because she had a horrible feeling that the battle of last night was only the beginning of a war between good and evil. It would be made even harder because they had no idea who or what the evil was.

Not everything was clear cut black and white. Like the jet black-eyed demon dragon. He was definitely different than all of the others. He had helped her escape, had killed his own brethren, but in the name of whatever he was pursuing.

She didn't think he was in command of the rest of the demon dragons. When she had encountered him in her apartment, it was more like he had slipped in with them. He didn't even look the same as they did, and Jakob said demon dragons didn't shift into men. But, there was no mistaking that she had seen him in the forest when she was on the train.

And what was up with her weird visions of the relic? They hadn't yet found it or the woman who now wore it as a necklace. Was she friend or foe?

Could she possibly be a mate like Ciara, or would she be the only one?

She hoped not. All of the dragon warriors that she had met deserved mates, deserved love.

Then there was her mother.

Sigh.

What was she going to tell her? Ciara could just imagine that conversation now.

"Hi mom. So I married a dragon."

"Ciara Mosley-Willingham, that is not acceptable."

End of conversation.

Maybe she'd be a wuss and let Wesley tell her mom she wasn't ever coming back. No, that certainly wasn't fair to him.

Jakob nuzzled her ear. "I can practically hear your brain working so hard it's about to ignite. What are you thinking about and is it all the dirty delicious things you want to do to me?"

"I have plenty of those ideas stored up. But what I'm trying to figure out now is how to tell my mother I am not coming back to work for her.

Jakob stopped mid-nibble down her neck. "You're not?"

"It'll be kind of hard to do that from rural Czech Republic."

"I didn't want to assume that you wanted to live there." He shifted so that Ciara lay on her back and could look up at him. "I made too many decisions in the beginning without talking to you and that was a mistake. There are green dragons all over the world. Although not many in this area. We can live anywhere. Just because the seat of the Green Dragon Wyr has been in the Slavic lands for thousands of years doesn't mean it always has to be."

"Well, we do need to find a new lair for your treasure." She knew he didn't want to leave his homeland, but she would make him squirm for just a few minutes. "I hear the middle of nowhere Nebraska has a large population of Czech people. They even have Nebraska Czech Days, where we can eat goulash and kledniki and kolaches." She only knew all of this because she'd had a young lady from Clarkson, Nebraska who needed to have a big fat Bohemian wedding.

"Sounds nice." Asshat had called her bluff.

"I don't want to move to Nebraska. We are going back to the villa and making it our home. But I wouldn't mind visiting here every once in a while." She punched him in the shoulder.

"Ow."

"Oh, sorry. I forgot that was your arm that the demon dragon munched on yesterday."

He grinned with a twinkle in his eye. "You'll just have to make that up to me."

She giggled and began kissing him everywhere. "You have ridiculously wide shoulders I'd like to run my lips along and maybe even nibble."

"Nobody is stopping you. But be careful. That's where I hide my wings."

She popped her head up. "Really?"

He chuckled and kissed the top of her head.

"No, wait. Really?"

He didn't answer her question, but instead grabbed Ciara at the waist and rolled so that she straddled him. "Isn't this where everything began?"

"Yes, we just need a little bit of hay to complete the picture." Ciara wrinkled her nose and wiggled it like she was Samantha from Bewitched. Long stalks of oat, barley, and wheat grains sprouted up all around the bed. They grew to full size within seconds and then dried to a crisp golden brown. There are only a few handfuls, but Jakob pulled them up in a handful and sprinkle them across the pillow. He saved two dry stalks and poked them into her hair.

"There. Perfect."

What was really perfect was the way they loved each other. Ciara gasped. She never told him. She had never said the words.

She placed her hands on his chest and leaned down to brush a gentle kiss across his lips. "I love you."

Jakob pushed a hand into her hair and groaned. "You have no idea how long I waited to hear you say that."

"Three or four days?"

"A lifetime." He kissed her back, not as demanding this time. He wasn't gentle with her, and she wouldn't want him to be, but this was different. It was a sealing of their souls. "I love you, Ciara."

Ciara lingered over the kiss a moment longer, savoring the taste of his love for her. Most of their lovemaking had been fast and furious, and she wanted this time to be special, to last.

She sat up and scooted back until she found just the right position. Jakob's cock was hard and ready for her, and she wanted to give him as much pleasure as he had given her.

This was the first time she'd gotten to really look at him. No wonder he'd filled her up so well each time he'd been inside of her. He was damn big. She demonstrated exactly how big by licking him from root to tip.

"While I have had fantasies about fucking your mouth, if you do very much of that I won't be able to hold out. And I need to take that hot pussy of yours. I need to come inside of you, make your scent my own. Claim you, mark you as my own."

She licked at him again this time taking the head of his cock into her mouth. His hips jerked and one of his hands went immediately into her hair.

"Fuck, baby. I take it back. Suck me. I'll fuck you as soon as I recover from this."

God, that was a turn on. She loved how much he wanted her. How much he was turned on by her. She swirled her tongue around and around the head, paying special attention to the little V underneath. Then she took him into her mouth as deep as she could go.

"Holy shit." His hand in her hair gripped tight, pulling at it, guiding her to suck his shaft, bobbing her head up and down. She loved the tingle across her scalp that his pull on her hair gave her. And she loved to hear his groans.

"Christ, Ciara. Where did you learn to suck cock like that? No, wait. Don't tell me. I don't want to know. Just take me in deep again like you did before."

She pushed his cock all the way to the back of her throat and swallowed, almost gagging herself. She was rewarded for that with a shuddered moan and a second hand in her hair. She did it one more time, then hollowed her cheeks as she pulled her mouth up his shaft and off of him.

She wanted to tease him more, suck on his balls while she stroked his shaft in her hand. But she didn't get a chance. Jakob hauled her up, dug one hand into her waist and grabbed his cock with the other.

"Ride me, Ciara. Now." He swiped his cock up and down her pussy, getting them both wet, and using it to play with her clit. That didn't last long though, before he positioned himself at her entrance and thrust up into her.

She hissed in a long breath feeling his cock stretch the inside of her, filling her completely. It only took a moment before she needed to move.

Ciara had never been on top before. Not like this. Never thinking a big girl could do this. Boy, was she wrong.

This position gave her all of the control, she could ride him anyway she wanted. And she wanted.

She slowly lifted her rear end and dropped it back down again. Oh yeah. That was it. Just like that.

She did that over and over until sweat beaded her upper lip and her thighs were on fire. But she couldn't stop. It felt too good, driving her so close to coming. She just needed a little more to ride over the top of that climax.

"Ciara, yes, fuck me." Jakob's hands slid up her sides, he grasped the soul shard she wore around her neck and for a moment they were completely one. She felt what he felt, he knew what she knew. Their souls were intertwined.

The moment lasted only seconds but, it would be ingrained in their very beings forever.

"I love every part of you, my curvy witch."

He cupped her breasts and pinched her nipples nice and hard. Spiking her closer and closer to coming. She rode him harder.

"Fuck, Ciara, I'm so close to coming. Come with me, baby. Milk my cock with your cunt." Jakob dropped one hand and slipped it between them. He found her clit and scissored his fingers over it.

Hell yeah. That shot her to the edge of her control. "Yes, Jakob yes. I love you. I love you."

Jakob threw back his head and his hips jerked. "Ciara, mate. Love you."

His words were the last thing she needed to topple over the edge into nirvana. She lost control of the rhythm of their bodies and came so hard that she saw stars. Colorful ones behind her eyelids. Jakob yelled her name over and over and shot his seed into her.

They came together, and they collapsed together. She was sure she was crushing him, but after that orgasm she couldn't move. He was a big strong dragon, he could survive having a chubby girl splayed out on top of him.

They laid together that way, breathing hard, hands stroking over each other's skin for a long time. When they had both floated back down to earth, Jakob lifted her face from under his chin and found her lips with his.

He was still buried inside of her and she didn't want to move yet. Jakob grabbed her ass and held her tight to his body. "I love you, Ciara. And I'm not just saying that because you blew my fucking mind. I love you. I want the whole world to know. Marry me. Throw the biggest most spectacular wedding you've ever planned, then stand with me in front of all of Dragonkind and your mother, and say you're mine."

"I am yours, whether we have a wedding or not. But I will stand up with you so that you can tell the whole world that your mine too. Tell everyone that we belong to each other."

She said yes with her words, and then she said yes with her body. All night.

She was a dragon's mate, a white witch, and the happiest she'd ever been.

She was in love.

DID you lurrve Jakob and Ciara's story? Keep reading with the next book in the series - Tease Me.

WANT to be the first to know when the next book in this series comes out (plus get cool exclusive content from me!)? Sign up for my Curvy Connection newsletter!

You'll get book release news, contests and giveaways, and exclusive previews and excerpts. You can also join my review team for free books!

A LETTER FROM THE AUTHOR - WHO LOVES DRAGONS?

Dear reader,

I hope you loved reading this first adventure in the Dragons Love Curves series with Ciara and Jakob as much as I loved writing it!

The dragons and their mates have a lot more adventures coming your way. So many questions to be answered. Who stole the First Dragon's relic, and who is Mrs. Bohacek really? What's up with the demon dragon dude who saved Ciara in the forest who thinks she owes him a favor? Who or what is behind all the bizarro things happening to the dragon warriors?

Keep reading the Dragons Love Curves series to find out and get your fix of sexy dragon shifters giving their mates happy ever afters (and happy endings! Lol)

Check out what happens next in *Tease Me*. Remember Steele? Yep, he's got some curves coming his way!

If you enjoyed the Dragons Love Curves books and you're ready for more paranormal romance, check out my Fated for Curves series - geek girls, bear-shifter space rangers and a strange town called Magic, New Mexico. Grab the first book in the series - *A Touch of Fate* today

I'd love to hear what's on your dirty little minds, so be sure to leave a review for this story. I really appreciate you telling other readers what you though.

Need more curvy girls getting their happy ever afters?

Sign up for my Curvy Connection mailing list.

You'll get book release news, contests and giveaways, and exclusive previews and excerpts. I'll send you another curvy girl romance book just to say thanks! You can even join my review team and get the next book before it's even released.

Find me at www.AidyAward.com or on Facebook, Twitter, Instagram, or follow me on BookBub.

Kisses,

~Aidy

EXCERPT FROM TEASE ME

Tease Me
A Dragons Love Curves Novel
Book Two

Fulfill a destiny, save the world and the soul of her mate.

Fleur Anthousai, a curvy earth witch, has known since birth
that she has a destiny to fulfill. Too bad nobody told her what
it was. She hopes her friends, the Troika wolf pack of Rouge,
New York, might have finally pointed her in the right
direction when she's invited to the multi-pack scenting
ceremony. Surely, becoming a wolf mate will set her on the
path to understanding her own prophecy.

Steele Zeleny is a green warrior dragon and he's damn good
at protecting the world from the darkness that is the demon
dragons, all while romancing the pants off any and all the
ladies. All bets are off when a shard of his soul demands that
the curviest, sexiest little flower of a witch is his true mate.

Fleur's destiny and Steele's soul are more important to the fate of the world than either of them know.

DUMB IDEA

This was the stupidest fucking idea ever. Skintight pants that tore off at the hips, nothing but suspenders above the waist, and a goddamn fireman's hat.

"Wooo hooo. Honey, take it off." A slightly older woman who was definitely the alpha female in the room whooped at them.

Steele leaned to the side to speak so only Daxton could hear. He fought to fake a smile for the ladies, but couldn't quite manage it, which was unusual. He'd always been able to charm the pants off any woman, anytime he liked.

His dragon wanted nothing to do with any of these ladies.

Weird.

The dragon part of him loved flirting, especially with beautiful women. Their soft luscious curves, the way they moaned when he licked them from head to toe, the way they came on his dick. Just not any of these screaming meamies.

"I'm going to kill you for talking me into wearing these costumes. You'll be a dragonskin rug in front of my fireplace come winter."

"You can murder me later. The Troika boys asked for our help. We might as well have some fun while we're doing it." Dax had his eyes on the rowdy red-head waving dollar bills like a lasso. He always did go for the brash and bawdy types.

Two minutes after they'd walked into the speak-easy, Konstatin Troika jumped at the chance of having two dragon warriors around. A pre-mating party, he'd called it, and promised a room full of horny women, who didn't need to know they were being guarded.

Steele didn't mind protecting the women while on his R&R. Combining work hard and play hard together was his specialty.

The Troika boys wanted the unmated women who were here for the special three-pack mating get together to have extra security. They just didn't want their mates knowing about it.

What Kosta hadn't said was that Steele and Dax were the entertainment.

Thank the First Dragon, Dax stepped forward and into the crowd of women all stuffed into this snack-sized apartment. They surrounded him with hoots and hollers sounding to him more like a pack of wolves than humans. At least half of them were shifter she-wolves, anyway.

Two women grabbed Steele's arms and pulled him into their circle, too, sliding their bodies up and down his, running their hands over his bare chest. Their touches did nothing for him but send a few creepy crawlies up his skin.

What the hell was wrong with him? This was the perfect opportunity. Beautiful women were literally begging him to take his clothes off, and he couldn't be less interested.

Steele had every intention of getting laid at least a couple dozen times on his week off, but maybe not all on the same night. These women were crazy and weren't doing it for him at all.

Which was worrying. He hadn't been turned off since he'd hit puberty. These last few years a fucking houseplant could turn him on.

Was his prime creeping up on him already?

No way. He wouldn't let it. A deep beat coupled with a tinny *psst psst psst* blared from the cheap portable stereo. He could shake his ass with the best of them. Time to get his flirt on.

Steele grabbed the closest woman at the hips and lifted her, wrapping her legs around his waist. He ground against her, hoping, waiting for his cock to join the god-damned party.

"Go, Zara, go, Zara." The women around him chanted and the lady in his arms turned firetruck red.

"Niko is going to go ballistic when he hears about this," she squealed.

"Good. A little jealousy will go a long way." The other woman dancing at his side, tried to grab his ass and laughed. "I love it when Max gets all possessive, the sex is amazing. So, me next."

Kosta had been right. These women were trouble with a capital T-R-O-U-B-L and E. He was down for having a good time, but he would never come between anyone and their mate. He danced with them for another minute and then spun both around and into a waiting couch. "Now, now ladies. Let the single girls have a chance, too."

"Spoilsport."

This party should be exactly what he needed, but tonight Steele would rather wrap himself around one soft cuddly woman. One who could warm his bed during the long winter months at his post at the Green Wyr stronghold.

The Czech winter was coming, and he didn't want to spend it alone.

Pretending to be strippers at a pre-mating party was not the way to find a mate.

Wait. Whoa, hold the phone. Mate? No fucking way.

Just because Jakob Zeleny, the head of his Wyr clan was the first dragon in more than a six-hundred years to find a true mate didn't mean the rest of them would, or could, or even should.

Nope. Steele was on the verge of hitting his Prime years. His glory days of carousing and bedding every woman he could would end too soon. He had to take every advantage of this vacation to get into as many dirty girl's panties as possible.

A goddess in a pink flowy top and tight jeans that hugged all her curves - and there were oh so many - walked into the room with a tray of drinks.

His eyes were instantly drawn to the green sparkling tree charm hanging from a chain just above her fantastic tits. He'd happily add both the charm and this hot curvy chick to his treasure trove. He tore his eyes from the necklace and drew his gaze down to the sweet sway of her hips and over her plump ass.

Fuck, yeah. Those were the exact panties he aimed to get into. He danced his way out of the group of women and over to his pink prey. She stopped beside him not attempting to take the cocktails into the pulsing crowd of women now surrounding Dax.

"Having fun, big boy?" A soft voice that sounded like ripe

peaches, a warm mountain sunrise, and butterfly wings lilted from her.

What the fuck did that even mean? He shook his head waiting for the momentary brain fart to pass.

"No?" She laughed, the sound tinkling like frozen bluebells.

Holy shit. His brain was broken.

He licked his lips and tried to speak. A low growl came out.

"Whoa. Sorry. I didn't know we paid for Grumpy Bear."

He was no bear. But she wasn't either. Her green eyes danced for him and sparkled brighter than her jewelry. They were the exact color of the field in front of his cabin in the spring after a rainstorm.

This was a wolf party, he inhaled her sweet scent looking for the nature of her shifter animal. She wasn't one of the wolves, but she wasn't a mere human. He stared into her eyes, searching for any clue, scenting her light arousal, trying to figure out what form she would take.

A fluffy bunny or a lovely plump doe. She had a soft look about her that he liked, but she was a little too smart-ass to be a carrot-eater. They were all gentle. She had a bite. Her scent teased all his senses.

A skunk maybe. Soft and docile, but also clever and ravenous.

He uncrossed his arms and shook them out. "No, little flower, you didn't pay for a grump, and I'm no bear."

"That I can see." She looked him up and down, taking her time, damn well drinking him in.

Oh, she had to be a hunter with that needy glint to her eye. He'd just been made into a piece of meat to her, he was positive of that. If he didn't know better he'd say she was part dragon.

But there was no such thing as a female dragon.

"And if you didn't notice. I'm not exactly little." There was both a bit of defiance and something else shy in her voice and eyes.

Yeah. He'd noticed. She had nice wide hips he could grab onto while he thrust into her, a thick ass he couldn't wait to squeeze, and plump tits he could get lost in for years.

Shit. He'd been too long without a woman. He'd gone from hello to growl to imagining fucking her brains out all inside of a minute. Well, minus the hello.

"I noticed every luscious inch of you, Flower."

Her eyes widened and she laughed, more than the tinkling giggle from before. This was hearty from the gut. The sound went straight into his balls and lifted his cock.

About time it fucking showed up.

"Do we have to pay extra for the fake flirtations or is that part of the service?"

Apparently he needed to up his game. "It wasn't fake. You're a beautifully fuckable woman I'd like to lick up and down until you're screaming from the pleasure."

There. That ought to do it.

She got the cutest crinkle between her eyes, blinked and shook her head like he'd said the most ridiculous thing she'd ever heard. Then she raised the tray of drinks and walked into the crowd.

"Okay, ladies. Who wants some of Galyna's marshmallow shots?" She tossed the words out, not giving him another look.

Every scale-covered fiber of his dragon-being wanted, no needed, to follow her. He wasn't one to go against his dragon.

Two steps forward and he was surrounded by three women who undulated and ground themselves against him.

"Oh my gawd. Look at these muscles," one woman said, pawing at his stomach.

"And those arms." Another woman lifted his arm and caressed his bicep. "Flex it for me."

His Flower was smiling and chatting, handing out drinks, and rolls of dollar bills to the twenty some-odd women. If he could just escape these fondlers he'd push through, take her away from all this, and get to know her. In a biblical sense.

He didn't know her name and couldn't call to her. He willed her to look at him with his mind. He was so damn close to calling up his dragon form, so he could simply speak into her mind.

She must have felt him staring at her because she looked up from her conversation. "I'm not paying you to stand around, grumpy. Shake that ass."

"What a tight ass it is." One of the fondlers ran a hand over his rear and pinched it.

He almost yelped. Holy crap. He was no sensitive-skinned baby, but damn. He was going to have a welt. These she-wolves were aggressive. Not that he minded a woman who went after what she wanted. Especially if *he* was what she wanted.

What he wanted right now was the pink bit of flesh peeking between Flower's shirt and her jeans as she bent over to set her tray on the table.

Oh, how he could bend her over that table.

He scooted away from pincher-lady, who must be a damn crab-shifter, and tried to get closer to Flower.

"Take it off, fireman. Let's see your hose." The Velcro

holding his pants together pulled, almost coming apart as the women clawed at him.

He pushed their hands away, his only focus on getting to his lady in pink. She handed out the last of her drinks, slid around the back of the couch, and circled around the group going back to the kitchen.

He stalked her movement with his eyes, loving the chase, and the slippery way she kept evading him. "You ladies are wearing me out. I think I need a drink."

Half a dozen women held up shot glasses made from marshmallows for him.

"Uh, thanks, but I'll grab some water." Steele followed his prey, into the soft light of the kitchen. Every counter top was covered in rows of herbs and greenery. More baskets hung over the sink and in the window. He'd left an apartment living room and entered a forest of edible greens. It was stunning, and his dragon reveled in the earthy scent of it all. She might really be a bunny shifter. One that he was going to hunt down and eat. In the fun way.

His Flower stood with her back to him, arranging cups of blue, red, and purple gloop on her tray. Finally, he had her alone.

"What is your name, little flower?

She jumped about three feet. "You scared me. Don't you know not to sneak up on a girl like that?" She downed one of the shots of goo, and then offered one to him. "I'm Fleur. I assumed you knew from the agency or something. I booked the strippers, I thought maybe my name was down as a contact or something.

He took her hand, set the cup down, and kissed her palm, then her wrist. A zing zipped through his lips, down his spine and straight to his cock.

"Oh, you shocked me." She giggled, but didn't pull her hand away.

He continued kissing up her arm, and then to her neck, touching the chain of the necklace. It glinted, calling to him. He licked the gold and her skin below.

"I don't know what you're doing or why you're doing it to me, but it feels amazing, don't stop." Fleur pushed her hands into his hair and gripped his scalp, urging him on.

Good thing these pants were tear away Velcro, because he wouldn't be able to wait very long to get inside her heat. He could scent the spike in her arousal, it pushed his own even higher.

She tilted her head to the side, giving him even more access. "If you didn't already know my name, why do you keep calling me flower?"

He nibbled his way up to her ear, then whispered, "Have you ever seen Bambi?"

"Sure." She sucked in a surprised breath and pushed him away. Her eyes got wide and then narrowed. "Oh my God. Is this your polite stripper way of telling me I smell? As in skunky?"

He laughed deep and hard. "No. In fact, you smell like springtime, and harvest, and green valleys, and snow-capped mountains."

"Wow. You are such a flirt. That agency rocks. I'll remember to request you for next year's pre-mating party. Although, I'll get a bit green, but you have got to kiss some of the other single girls here like that. Big tips will definitely get shoved down your pants. In fact, you should check with Zara to see if she can get you a job at The Sleepy Folk. With your flirting skills you'd get lots of tips from all the cougars."

He may not ever put his lips on another woman's flesh ever again. "I am not flirting with you. I am seducing you."

"Do you get a bonus if we request you by name? What's your name? Ooh, wait, do guys have stripper names, too? I'll bet yours is cinnamon, no wait, honey buns."

"I don't belong to any agency, I don't need a job, and I'm not a stripper. My name is Steele."

"That's a perfect stripper name. Wait. You're not from the agency? Are you freelance? I didn't know that was a thing."

Steele stepped closer, pushing her lush body against the counter. He set a hand on either side, caging her in.

"I am not a stripper, little flower. I am a dragon."

Get your copy of Tease Me on Amazon.
Click here to get your copy now
or get it for free with your KU subscription.

ALSO BY AIDY AWARD

The Curvy Love Series

Curvy Diversion

Curvy Temptation

Curvy Persuasion

Curvy Domination (coming soon)

The Curvy Seduction Saga

Rebound

Rebellion

Reignite

Dragons Love Curves

Chase Me

Tease Me

Bite Me

Cage Me

Baby Me

Defy Me

More dragons coming soon!

Fated for Curves

A Curvy Girl Sci-fi Romance Series

A Touch of Fate

A Tangled Fate

A Twist of Fate

More Space Rangers coming soon!

ABOUT THE AUTHOR

Aidy Award is a curvy girl who kind of has a thing for stormtroopers. She's also the author of the popular Curvy Love series and the hot new Dragons Love Curves series. She writes curvy girl erotic romance, about real love, and dirty fun, with happy ever afters because every woman deserves great sex and even better romance, no matter her size, shape, or what the scale says.

Read the delicious tales of hot heroes and curvy heroines come to life under the covers and between the pages of Aidy's books. Then let her know because she really does want to hear from her readers.

Connect with Aidy on her website. www.AidyAward.com get her Curvy Connection, and join her Facebook Group - Aidy's Amazeballs.

Made in the USA
Coppell, TX
25 January 2024

28159978R00155